In the Cemetery of the Orange Trees

ALSO BY JEFF TALARIGO

The Pearl Diver
The Ginseng Hunter

As much a book of poetry as a novel, as much a symphony as a memoir, this is an extraordinary book from a writer at the top of his powers. Reminiscent of Berger and Calvino, Jeff Talarigo manages to capture the breadth and circumference of story-telling, while also giving us a privileged insight into the daily life and dreams of Gaza.

–Colum McCann, *Thirteen Ways of Looking*

What Jeff Talarigo has accomplished here is quite remarkable. *In the Cemetery of the Orange Trees* captures with poignancy and precision the harrowing effect of the Occupation on the lives of those who endure it. In the terms of the novel itself, I would rate this a 'five cigarette' story.

–James Shapiro, Professor of English, Columbia University

Jeff Talarigo's storyteller prefaces his stories with a warning: "We are all exaggerators of the truth, stretchers of stories, sometimes outright liars even. But our exaggerations, our stretches, our lies, are ours and that is why we must believe them, for they are the only things we can call our own." *In the Cemetery of the Orange Trees* is a collection of such stories of decades of strife and life in the Gaza region. The stories are told in the manner of Aesop or Orwell, allegorically and mythologically familiar, but in Talarigo's prose they soar. Violence, inhumanity and sadness are challenged by hope, forgiveness, appreciation, loyalty, and rebellion. And we must believe them.

–David S. Ferriero, Archivist of the United States

Thanks be to Jeff Talarigo for his immense humanity, his literary gift for imaginative presence and witness, his absorption, creation and weaving of pungent stories which make Palestine/Gaza feel as haunting and real as they truly are. Here we feel, in potent, amplified form, the sorrowing presences of our extended human families who suffered outrageous injustice for whole generations, and it still goes on. Jeff is a crucial witness: what he does in this exquisite, mysterious text is make a whole world come alive.

–Naomi Shihab Nye, *Habibi* and *19 Varieties of Gazelle*

in the
Cemetery
of the
Orange Trees

JEFF TALARIGO

Etruscan Press

Etruscan Press
Wilkes University
84 West South Street
Wilkes-Barre, PA 18766
(570) 408-4546

W
WILKES UNIVERSITY

www.etruscanpress.org

Published 2018 by Etruscan Press
Printed in the United States of America
Cover design by Carey Schwartzburt
Interior design and typesetting by Susan Leonard
The text of this book is set in Chapparal Pro.

First Edition

17 18 19 20 5 4 3 2 1

Library of Congress Cataloguing-in-Publication Data

Names: Talarigo, Jeff, author.
Title: In the cemetery of the orange trees / by Jeff Talarigo.
Description: First edition. | Wilkes-Barre, PA : Etruscan Press, [2018]
Identifiers: LCCN 2017014816 | ISBN 9780997745542 (softcover)
Subjects: LCSH: Palestinian Arabs--Fiction. | Culture conflict--Fiction. |
   BISAC: FICTION / Literary. | FICTION / Family Life. | FICTION / Political.
   | GSAFD: Allegories.
Classification: LCC PS3620.A525 I5 2018 | DDC 813/.6--dc23
LC record available at https://lccn.loc.gov/2017014816

Please turn to the back of this book for a list of the sustaining funders of
Etruscan Press.

This book is printed on recycled, acid-free paper.

For the people of Jabaliya, and
for my father.

Seal me with your eyes.

Take me wherever you are—

Mahmoud Darwish

Table of Contents

So That We Never Forget   17

A Two Cigarette Story   27

The Night Guardian of the Goat   37

A Three Cigarette Story   53

The Boy Who Sold Martyrs   61

A Four Cigarette Story   83

My Father, the Mole   97

Border Shearing   119

As Far As One Can Go   167

Acknowledgments

So many have helped make this book possible.

From the Ohio years: Jack Hoover, Roger Gochneaur, Bill Currin and Barb McFarland—for being beams of light in those darkest of days.

To all the people in block number four in Jabaliya, especially the Elakra family and to Fayez, Bassam, Uncle Ali, Mustafa and Shafiq el Biss—for allowing me to see Gaza with my own eyes and for changing my life.

To the New York Public Library's Cullman Center for Scholars and Writers class of 2006–2007, for giving me the greatest year a writer could hope for. Thanks in particular to the following fellows for their guidance and unwavering support: Jim Shapiro, Jim Miller, Maya Jasanoff and David Blight. Also, to Jean Strouse, the glue that keeps everything together, and Pamela Leo, Adriana Nova, Betsy Bradley, Sam Swope, Miriam Gloger and David Ferriero. And to my cousins, Bill Schierberl and Margaret Pomeroy—New York is a much emptier place without you.

All those in my Boston years: the wonderful people at Grub Street, Theresa Tobin at MIT Library, AGNI, for publishing a part of this book and for the careful eye of Jennifer Alise Drew, to a couple of early readers and listeners, Dana Sadji and Reema Tambosi, and to the greatest book-store in the world—The Harvard Coop—a sanctuary where much of this was written.

All the students, past and present, and to the faculty at Wilkes University's Low-Residency MA/MFA Program who have provided an enormous amount of feedback and encouragement. Mike Lennon for his suggestion to bring the American into the novel; Bonnie Culver for passing this manuscript along and to three late-stage readers, Kevin Oderman, Teresa Loeffert, and Bev Donofrio.

Everyone at Etruscan Press for their care, bravery and passion for this book: Phil Brady, Bob Mooney, Bill Schneider, Pamela Turchin, Danielle Watson, Bob Antinozzi, Susan Leonard and Carey Schwartzburt.

And finally, to my mother, my father-in-law, Tadashi Toshimitsu, my wife, Aya, and son, Sam, who have also carried this book along with them for so many years.

In the Cemetery of the Orange Trees

JEFF TALARIGO

He has come here, to the land of the forgotten, in order that he may forget, that within their story he may perhaps find his.

⌁

His first hour there.

He appears in the city square on a February afternoon, unbeknownst to anyone, a backpack stooping his shoulders. Standing along Salah el Din Street, eating a falafel sandwich, eyes of curiosity are on the stranger, eyes of distrust, but they turn from him and down the street in an instant to where a convoy of soldiers approaches. Above him, unseen, a group of boys lurk on the rooftop, the stones in their hands itch their palms, and when the first jeep is within range they throw them. A loud bang and then another against the side of a jeep startle the stranger. Within seconds the soldiers are shooting at the boys and he, frozen, is caught in the crossfire. There is an alleyway behind him and he escapes into it. People are shouting, throwing anything they get their hands on: rocks, bottles, bananas, a water pipe. An old man yanks off his left shoe and fires it into the throng of soldiers. He watches the old man hobble away, leaving the shoe in the middle of the street. A soldier in the back of a jeep aims his Kalashnikov and shoots dead the shoe.

⌁

There is much the American does not know.

That one should never stand beneath the roof where stone throwers are perched. When soldiers pass, make yourself invisible. The waft of tear gas that seared his lungs earlier in the day is produced only forty miles from his hometown. Don't drink the last of the coffee in your glass. As of late, soldiers have been appearing on the streets, out of uniform, allowing them to get closer to the stone throwers. Sometimes they carry a backpack with a gun inside and then make arrests. The name Jabaliya means people of the mountain, and it is pronounced in even syllables – Ja – ba – li – ya.

⌐

This is where he wants to go—the largest camp in the Gaza Strip, the birthplace of the intifada, the uprising. He has no idea how to get there, or if he can even enter the place, only that it is north. Knowing that the sea is a mile away and to the west, he begins to walk through the city, keeping, as best he can, the sea to his left.

⌐

He hasn't been walking long before a voice, in his language, stops him.
  "What are you doing here?"
  "I want to go to Jabaliya," he says, mispronouncing the word.
  The young man corrects his pronunciation.
  "My name is Fayez. That is where I live."

⌐

Several hours later the two of them are walking up School Street and the American is gazing at the expanse of cement block houses. Children get close and Fayez tells them that the man is an American.
  "Go away," Fayez says to the children. They scatter for a second or two, but are back, appearing from everywhere, out of nowhere.
  "It's okay," the American says, removing his backpack and playing with the children.
  And this is how it is the entire way up School Street. Women poke their heads out of colorful doors, men sitting along the cement wall nod to the stranger.
  Nearing the house, the American asks:
  "Why is it that you are bringing me to your family?"
  Fayez watches the American shaking hands with the children and he smiles and says: "I trust your eyes."

⌐

So That We Never Forget

As of late, in the coastal village of al-Jiyya, there has been an increase in the sightings of the talking jackals. Ghassan, a fishing boat repairman, has lived his twenty-four years in a cave, just outside this village, which is equal distance from the two ancient coastal cities. He calls the cave *The Finger of Allah*, imagining that Allah, one day, poked his finger into the side of the mountain and created it. The cave has a beautiful view of the Sea and in it, on this late September day in 1948, is Ghassan's wife, eight months pregnant. From the entrance of the cave, standing at its far-right side and on her toes, Ghassan's wife can see the top of her husband's work hut down along the beach. It has been a while since she has done so because being anywhere near the bright sunlight sends flashes of pain into her head. Most of her days are spent at the rear of the cave, where only the final minutes of sunset can cast their auburn glow.

On this particular evening, as Ghassan is about halfway up the hill leading to his home, two jackals stand blocking the path. Ghassan continues walking toward them, and when he is fifteen feet away, one of the jackals speaks.

"I hear that your wife will soon have her first child."

"Yes, that is so."

"How wonderful for the both of you," the jackal says.

"Thank you. Now, could you let me pass? I must go and attend to my wife."

"We have just visited her and she looks very tired. Before we allow you to pass, there is something you must agree to help us with."

"What is it you want?" asks Ghassan.

The smallest of the jackals hands Ghassan a scroll of paper.

"We hear you are good with the brush and we need those names painted on signs for us. One name per sign."

Ghassan unrolls the scroll and looks at the long list of names.

"There must be over one hundred and fifty names here."

"Your mind is very quick. There are one hundred and seventy-six."

"It is in the script of the jackals. This will take weeks to do."

"No, they must be finished before your wife gives birth. If they are not completed by that time, your wife will give birth to a goat."

Ghassan looks at the jackals and can't believe what he is hearing.

"Where will I get all the wood for the signs?"

"It is all waiting for you by your home."

"And the paints?"

"So too are the paints."

"And how am I to learn this script?"

"Get practicing."

They step aside in order that Ghassan can pass. He quickly walks by and before he has made it around the bend, one of the jackals shouts, "You should hurry! It looks as though your wife may give birth early!"

—

Ghassan sees the hill of blank wooden signs in front of his home. There are two stacks, both taller than he. Next to the stack of signs is a barrel of paint. Simple white. He takes one of the signs and rubs his hand over its smooth surface. Each sign is a yard long. Ghassan does a quick calculation; four signs an hour, twenty signs each night. That would be more than a week, nine days to be exact, to complete them all.

He enters the cave and goes to the back where his wife is on her side, rubbing her stomach. She has told him how she can feel the hiccups of the baby and Ghassan finds this both miraculous and frightening. Only once has he even touched her stomach and it reminded him of an inflated balloon and how it cracks and becomes perilously taut when you paint it. Her eyes are open and she is looking at Ghassan. He thinks of asking her about the jackals, but decides against it. Stress, he has heard from the midwife, can cause a woman to go into labor early.

"How is your headache?"

"It is not bad today. For some reason the sunlight is not so strong. Is it cloudy?"

"Not a cloud," Ghassan catches himself, thinking of the stacks of wood and how they are probably blocking much of the bright sunlight.

"Not a cloud this morning, but as the day passed, more clouds began appearing."

"Have you anything for dinner?"

"I brought home some sardines and I will cook them and make bread as well."

Ghassan goes to the front of the cave and does what he has told his wife he would do. Soon there is dinner, which his wife only picks at.

"You must eat more."

"I have little appetite. I think the baby will come soon."

Ghassan gags on the fish bone of his wife's words.

"Eat some bread," his wife tells him.

He does as she says, although he knows there is no bone in his throat. He finishes his dinner and hurries outside and stirs the paint, looks at the long list of names on the sheet. He begins; the Hebrew script, although different, is at least in the same direction as his language—right to left. QIRYAT EQRON. YAD MORDEKHAY. ZIQIM. One by one, with hands weighted by a mortified heart and pounds of sadness, he paints the renamed towns and villages that have fallen in the war. But what is one to do, faced with the burden of being the father of a goat?

It is past midnight and Ghassan has completed twenty-two signs. He can barely lift his arm and he joins his wife on the mat. She sleeps and he thinks of reaching out and touching her stomach, but is afraid to, so he slides down the mat to where his head is level with her stomach and listens closely for the hiccups of their baby.

-≤-

The days that follow are the same; Ghassan goes off to work along the beach, rushes home, eats, then paints two dozen signs before wearily crawling onto the mat. He has seventy signs remaining; three more nights at his present pace. When he awakens, although tired, the knowledge that he is only a few days from completing the work gives Ghassan some energy. He steps out of the cave and rubs his eyes, trying to shake away the mirage before him. Overnight, another stack of signs has appeared with a new list of an additional six or seven dozen names nailed to them.

Ghassan doesn't go to work on this day and he paints nonstop; his only break is at dusk when the mosquitoes are at their most ravenous. By the time he makes it to his mat he has nearly completed the entire initial list given to him by the jackals. He sleeps little on this night and his wife tries to find a position that will allow her to rest. Ghassan dreams that his wife, while trying to leave the cave in the morning, is unable to do so, not because of the stacks of unpainted signs, although they do hinder her, but because her stomach has grown so large that it is like a massive boulder plugging the mouth of the cave. Ghassan is left with no choice but to deliver the baby himself; the screams of his wife can be heard for miles along the shoreline, mistaken by some as a foghorn, and then, after the baby is born, he must wait until his wife's stomach deflates enough for him to squeeze out of the cave. In this dream, he wakes feeling not the hiccups of the baby but the kicks, not one little leg kicking, or two, but four, and Ghassan bolts from the mat fearing that the time is near and, if he doesn't hurry, he will be the father of a goat.

As with all the signs he has painted, the five dozen he finished the day before are gone, taken away in the middle of the night. But today, as with yesterday, there is a new stack with a new list of names attached to it. He begins working on them at once and it is more of the same for the next couple of days; Ghassan is unable to go down to his work hut.

On the twelfth day of sign-painting, Ghassan's wife lets out a scream and she screams again and again. Her water has broken and Ghassan, before spinning and running down the hill in search of the midwife, looks at the unfinished stack of signs, perhaps eighty are left, and he doesn't know what to do and he just stands there, locked in indecision and fatigue.

"Hurry, Ghassan," his wife shouts. "It feels like a horse is coming out!"

These words kick Ghassan down the hill and to the village of al-Jiyya where the midwife lives. He races past his work hut and along the break-wall and to the village. He is yelling for the midwife, but no one comes out of their houses. The village is without sound, not a single man gurgling from a waterpipe or sipping morning coffee, not a single person in their house. The village's six dairy cows are nowhere to be seen.

Ghassan retraces his steps. At the village entrance he notices, above his head, one of the signs he has painted—MOSHAV GE'A. Briefly he admires his work before wondering where the sign for his village—al-JIYYA—has gone. But he knows. He knows what he has done, his betrayal.

He thinks of his wife and passes the breakwall and his work hut and several fishing boats in disrepair. As he is about to turn onto the path leading to his cave, Ghassan hears the bleating of a goat. He imagines the goat is still sticky in its birth fluids, wobbling on newborn legs. Ghassan turns from the path and hurries southward knowing that by following the shoreline, in a few hours, he will come to the city of Gaza.

⟋

But it is the conscience of man that makes him different from animals, is it not? Would a wolf or a bird or a horse be pestered the further it moved away from its pregnant mate? Perhaps the animal would return out of instinct, but guilt would not prey on its mind rendering it unable to go a step further.

It is this guilt that forms a sheen on our skin and takes an enormous, debilitating effort on our part to shed. And it is this that turns Ghassan around, halfway to Gaza. He retraces his footsteps past the fallen villages, past the signs that he has painted, and up that hill he has climbed thousands of times, but never as difficult as on this day, and he comes to the mouth of his cave and in there lies a baby goat, lapping at its birth fluids. Ghassan looks around, inside the cave and out, for his wife. He calls her name. Only the cave answers. The goat glances at him and Ghassan wonders, if like infants, newborn animals also cannot see clearly.

Ghassan bends down, lifts and cradles the baby goat, walks out of the cave for the last time in his life, down the hill and along the beach, south with the sun on the left side of his face, atop his head, and onto the right. Before the sun drowns itself in the Sea, as he arrives at the

Gaza border, with a city of tent camps swelling the beach, Ghassan lifts the tiny, floppy ear of the goat and whispers into it a promise, a promise of remembrance, that same promise that each and every generation of goat will whisper into their kids' tiny ears. On and on, so that they never forget.

⁓

Much of the time in those early days they keep the American in the house, for his safety as well as theirs. Each day they take a walk up and down School Street, sometimes, for a short while, they sit against the wall across the way.

Inside he whittles away the plodding climb and descent of the days. For the most part he stays in the back room, where the men sleep. In his notebooks he writes what he hears: of the footsteps in the alleyway, of cars and donkey carts passing up and down the street, the calls to prayer, the thrum of voices speaking words he does not understand.

At night, while the others are asleep, he eavesdrops on the sounds, imagining what it is like out there during curfew, where, he has been told, that if one is caught they are arrested or shot. Sometimes he hears voices from the neighboring houses or a television or radio.

Often on these nights, while finding it difficult to sleep, he hears Bassam, the eldest brother, get up and go from the sleeping room, where there are six men on mats side by side, from wall to wall. Bassam goes into the common room and paces. The American has heard from others, although not from Bassam himself, that Bassam has spent more than eleven months in prison; the American wonders if this is why he cannot sleep. The American listens to the sliding feet, then the pause when Bassam stops and lights a cigarette, again the pacing. In and out of sleep he fades, waking to the sound of shuffling feet.

—

Shafiq, the only veterinarian in Gaza, introduces the American to his grandfather, Zajil, a famous storyteller well into his eighties, who only tells stories when paid by cigarettes. Each time the American visits the old man he brings with him a pack of cigarettes. He lights one and hands it to Zajil and, like that, for a short, magical time, coherent words and stories are once again a part of his life.

Before Zajil tells the American his stories, he begins with the same words:

"We are all exaggerators of the truth, stretchers of stories, sometimes outright liars even. But our exaggerations, our stretches, our lies, are ours and that is why we must believe them, for they are the only things we can call our own."

A Two Cigarette Story

I was twelve, not eleven as I had once thought, when my grandfather
first took me to the cemetery of the oranges.

We had just finished lunch and my grandfather told me to come
with him to the market. I thought nothing of it, for I had gone there
with him on many occasions, but when we walked up School Street,
away from the market, I wanted to say something, but I did not.

It was at that time of year, late autumn, when the leaves of the
giant willow began to turn a crinkled brown. I hated that season when
the tree lost its green umbrella, the time when we most needed its
protection from the cold, rainy months of January and February. As we
passed the garbage bins, I ignored the goats that were nibbling through
the rubbish, the same goats that my friends and I threw small stones at,
imagining they were soldiers.

We came to the end of School Street to where one could either turn
left or right. Before us, the fractured remains of what once was the
railroad that ran from the great cities of the Ottoman Empire, through
Gaza, all the way across the north of Africa to Morocco.

It was beyond theses tracks, however, that lay something much
more important: a place I and most of the children in the camp were
forbidden to go. Stories varied from family to family as to why we
shouldn't cross these tracks; two boys, my age, were playing there with
an unexploded cluster bomb when it detonated and killed the both of
them; a girl, the daughter of a sheik, was last seen crossing into the
field, never to be seen again; it was a sacred place, where the corpses of
thousands of orange trees lay.

My grandfather stared down at me, his bent, black-framed glasses
made his dark eyes smaller than when he drew his sketches in
his notebook without them. He took my hand and we looked both
ways along the rusty tracks as if the trains had last passed by that
morning and not forty years before. We climbed the slight incline,
him with his limp, and over the tracks.

We continued along in the field skirting the north end of the camp and soon, after crossing several dusty knolls, we arrived at a place tucked behind a knot of acacia shrubs. I stopped, as did my grandfather, when I saw the glorious blue swath of the sea. I had, of course, been to the sea, only two miles away, but from there in the field, from that distance, I had never seen it so blue and with those blinking eyelashes of white.

So distracted, I didn't notice the small group of men sitting in a circle around a snapping fire. We walked down the hill and my grandfather greeted the men, all, I could see, were older than him, which surprised me for my grandfather was perhaps the oldest person I knew. Several of the men sat on old plastic chairs, others on flattened boxes, and they all shifted clockwise to make space for the both of us. My grandfather and I shared a piece of cardboard and when we sat I could no longer see the sea.

The wind agitated the fire and I gazed into its agitation. No one said anything until one of the men, a spindly man with a scatter of teeth, reached into his worn jacket and held out two cigarettes, splayed in his hand like the "V" for victory sign we flashed the soldiers. He held the cigarettes like that, his hand trembling. Another man and then another did the same until all the men, except my grandfather, were holding out two cigarettes. My grandfather reached into his robe and unfolded a red handkerchief and placed it on the ground where each of the men tossed their cigarettes; one edge of the handkerchief blew overtop them. My grandfather leaned over and folded the remaining ends of the handkerchief and left it sitting there.

He began to talk:

"As a child growing up in the Hula Valley I was always shooting small stones at the birds with my slingshot. The stones were too tiny to kill the birds, I never wanted to kill them, but if I hit them in the correct spot, the head or maybe the proper crease in the wing, I could stun them just long enough for me to run over and touch them. I loved the feel of their soft, yet taut feathers, their oily heads and tiny claws digging their fear into my palm. The only way that I could touch them was if I hurt them a little.

"One day I hit a small bird in the head and it fell from an olive tree and lay unmoving in the dirt. I picked up the injured bird, and after a few minutes, I tried to release it into the sky, but it was injured so badly it couldn't fly away.

"Not knowing what to do, I took the tiny brown bird into the grain storage bin, which sat at the back of our house. Each day after working in the fields I would run home and feed it water and pieces of grain by hand. I did this for about a week and still the bird was unable to fly. One day, a Friday, I snuck a piece of string from my mother's sewing basket and tied it around the bird's claw. Its thin neck throbbed. The string was about a yard long and when I threw the bird into the air it would try flapping its wings, but soon the string ran out, and the bird would be yanked backward and left suspended, upside down, in mid-air, the string in my hand.

"My best friend, Nawaf, loved to watch the helpless bird, and after seeing his reaction, I decided to try and get more of these birds and sell them. I spent all my free time with the slingshot looking for birds. I used bigger stones to shoot the birds down, killing some in the process, but finally I had five birds like the first, too injured to fly away. I took five more pieces of string and went to the other villages trying to sell the birds. One boy from the neighboring village was angry and said that three mil was too much and that he would go and shoot his own birds. The argument turned into a fight and it brought a woman out of her house, and she broke it up. The woman happened to know my mother, and the next time she saw her at the market, she told her what I had been doing. That night, my mother took me onto the roof of the house and lectured me on how I should treat all of Allah's creations.

"She then made me kneel in our stony courtyard and recite sura 4:19 from the Koran: 'Allah forgives those who commit evil in ignorance and then quickly turn to Him in repentance. Allah will pardon them. Allah is all-knowing and wise. But He will not forgive those who do evil and, when death comes to them, say; Now we repent!'

"I repeated this sura until the moon dropped behind the date palms."

The dying fire was the only voice when my grandfather stopped. I sat there listening to the life of the fire, which spoke in the cadence of poetry. Reaching out, my grandfather picked up the handkerchief and placed it in his pocket. He stood, as did I, and said goodbye to the men.

Once out of the field he spoke the only words to me since we left our house: "It is in the cemetery of the orange trees that we keep alive our story."

We continued through block number six and I saw a cluster of pigeons flying by, reminding me of the birds in the story; I thought of asking my grandfather about the birds in his story and what happened to them, but like earlier in the day, I said nothing. We ended up at the western end of the market. My grandfather held my hand, but then, when we came to the butcher's he let go, leaving a chilled sheen of sweat on it.

Staring at me with huge bulbous eyes was a sheep's head; eyes so much like glass that I wanted to reach out and touch them. But the longer I met the eyes the more I thought that they were like ice rather than glass—cold to the touch, unlike glass which holds the warmth the longer one keeps their hand against it.

Then, in the reflection of the sheep's eye, I saw the red of my grandfather's handkerchief. I spun and looked at him. He unfolded the handkerchief, revealing the cigarettes, which looked like the whitest fingers I had ever seen—sixteen of them.

The butcher took all but one of the cigarettes and he went to the cage that held the squawking chickens. As the man opened the cage, it became difficult, if not impossible, to tell the individual chickens from the frantic flock. By the neck, the butcher grabbed one and held it up and my grandfather nodded in approval and before I knew what had happened, the knife, which I hadn't even seen, severed the head from the body. By the claws the butcher held the chicken, the stream of blood draining onto the ground until it slowed like the water dripped into the basin that I stood in on my Friday night showers.

My grandfather took the chicken by the claws and handed me the head, which the butcher had placed in a small waxed bag. Walking up School Street, halfway up the block, I turned and saw pellets of blood plunk, plunk, plunking into the beige dust.

Only then did I connect that it was Thursday; the one day each week when we ate meat. And on other Thursdays my grandfather would sometimes take me with him to the cemetery of the oranges and, for the rest of my life, I would remember the stories by the number of cigarettes the men would give to my grandfather. After dinner on those nights my grandfather would go outside in front of the house and smoke a cigarette, smoke it to the tips of his callused fingers.

That night, I stood behind him and he asked me, without turning around:

"Have you ever seen a shooting star, Shafiq?"

"No, Grandfather, I haven't."

"Keep your eyes to the sky."

I did and soon freckles of red sparks raced through the night air.

"Did you see them, Shafiq? Did you see the stars?"

"Yes. They were beautiful," I answered, even though I knew that it was only my grandfather flicking the cigarette high into the air, for I had seen him do so on many nights when he didn't know I was watching.

Then, as my grandfather did each night, he locked the green metal door behind him, keeping out the raven black shroud of curfew, until the next morning when, from atop the minaret, the muezzin would take a deep breath and cry out the call to prayers, releasing us into the streets for yet another day.

Awake before dawn, he quietly unbolts the door and steps onto School Street. A fog has settled overnight, rendering the willow nearly invisible. The school, fifty yards away, cannot be seen. He walks up the street and turns into the first alley, making his way through the labyrinth of block number four. He knows he mustn't stay long, but the pull of being alone, of seeing with his own eyes, is too much. The rush throttles him.

In the fog, the voice of the muezzin sounds as though it is being pressed through a sieve. The American stops and listens to the call to prayer, watches as sleepy men leave their houses to answer it. He says good morning to a man with a cane and the man lifts the walking stick in greeting. Years since he has felt so free.

At the end of his first week in Jabaliya, he asks for a razor and Fayez tells him that his uncle is a barber and later that night he would shave him.

It is around seven o'clock and the American is sitting on a chair in the middle of the room, a face full of shaving cream and a straight-edge being lowered to his neck. Neighbors and curious onlookers gather. Several dozen watch the initial slide of the blade plow a path along his neck. No one is talking; the crackle of week-old stubble explodes in the hush. The only light in the large room is a single bulb above the two men. The foreigner has large, dark eyes, appearing even more so against the white of the shaving cream. With these eyes he gives the barber a side glance:

"Do you realize how much I trust you?"

Fayez translates and there is a smatter of laughter.

"Yes," says the barber, "we understand that."

Again, the scratch of the blade exposes more of the pale flesh. Everyone watches as the barber wipes the blade on the towel draped over his shoulder. The eyes follow the blade back down and to another sweep of the neck and back to the towel and the neck again. Entranced by the rhythm, they wait for a tiny speck of red to bubble out from beneath the puffy white cloud of shaving cream.

It doesn't.

The man's face is clean, younger than most anticipate; a face perhaps, that with a little more sunshine, could be that of a soldier, or a stone thrower.

The crowd of onlookers begins to scatter and head back to their houses where, in a quarter of an hour, they will latch their doors and dim their lights and surrender to the hours of curfew.

⌐

Now, most mornings, after the call to prayer and before the morning session of school begins, children gather near the house and sneak beneath the white tarp that hangs there. They huddle outside the red metal door and whisper in chorus the American's name. Soon, the slide of the bolt clicks and the door opens and, for a short while, he talks to the children.

⌐

The Night Guardian of the Goat

For a single month, from new moon to new moon, I was the night guardian of the goat. It was a rather simple job, once one got used to the staying awake through the night and following the goat wherever his whims took him: garbage bin to garbage bin, under the willow, or simply to the house where his master, Ghassan Abu Majed, slept away the eight hours and thirty minutes of curfew.

It was exactly in that house, number eighty-eight in block six, in the front room across from the bathroom and kitchen, that the last remaining goat of Ghassan Abu Majed stayed for most of his ten years. A pretty good life for a goat, I imagine. It remained as such until Ghassan's wife of nearly half a century bolted the door at 7:55 the night before the April new moon, leaving the animal to butt his head against the door until he became tired and fell asleep outside. When Ghassan limped into the dawn air on his way to morning prayers, he nearly tripped over the goat, lying with his legs curled under, his hooves hidden in the fur of his belly.

Before Ghassan turned around, about to scold his wife for forgetting the goat outside, she spoke to him from the doorway.

"Our grandson is allergic to that beast. The child has been sniffling and coughing since the moment he was born."

Ghassan held his tongue, respecting the calm hovering over early morning, but the word *beast* rankled him. He bent over and stroked the goat's beard until the repetition kneaded away his anger.

"He is the last link to the land."

"The link has long been severed," she answered, in a voice also respectful of the hour and of her husband and the goat.

Ghassan balanced himself with his left hand and stood, slowly unfolding his aching limbs. He said nothing more to his wife and headed toward the peace of the mosque. The dust of the camp settled on his sandaled feet, but he ignored it, for he would wash them before prayers.

It was on that very afternoon that Ghassan asked me if I would be the night guardian of the goat. Jobless for more than a year, I said yes.

"Good," he said. "Now go and get some sleep, your work will begin tonight."

I went to his house at 7:30 and was given only one order.

"Don't ever allow the goat to speak or come into contact, in any way, with the soldiers."

I thought it rather strange that Ghassan used the word "speak," but I let it pass, for I assumed it to be merely a slip of the tongue. He left me with that message and closed the door, and the goat and I looked at each other and began to walk together up the darkening street. In the pink grapefruit glow of the setting sun, the military watchtower, the tallest structure in the camp, smirked down on us.

―

That first night, in fact the entire first week, the goat did nothing other than what one thinks a goat would do—sniff through the multitude of possibilities in the garbage on Jabaliya's streets. That was how we spent the majority of our time: I simply braced my back against a wall while the goat nosed around until he found a tasty morsel. I would listen to and sometimes watch the goat work his jaws, nostrils wet and splaying in rhythm, until the food was mashed enough so that it could easily slide down his throat. Sometimes he would stare at me watching him and I would remember what Ghassan had said. On several occasions, I thought the goat was about to speak, but I laughed at myself for allowing sleepiness to grapple with my imagination.

So it was, the nights passing in near silence, the sickle of the moon growing to half, giving the goat a cleaner white coat than in the harsh reality of the sun.

―

The quiet allowed much time for thought: of my only son wasting away his youth in an unknown prison for an unknown amount of time, while the moon I watch, then the nineteenth moon since I last saw him, goes about as it always has. But the goat was a distraction. A goat that has divided the people of Jabaliya into two groups—those who believe in its sacredness, the fifth generation of goats from the village of al-Jiyya, the fourth generation living here in this camp, and those for whom the goat is only a bitter, humbling reminder of what once was and never will be again.

And which side do you fall on, I asked myself. A good question, but I am afraid my answer was trapped somewhere in the abyss between trying to forget what happened to my people and trying never to forget. That began to change on my twelfth night with the goat.

About two-thirds of the way through curfew, the goat looked up at me from the wilted leaf of lettuce it was nibbling on.

"Pssst." The goat pointed his nose down the street.

I must say that I was startled, and had to place both hands against the ground to keep myself steady. When I continued to stare at the goat and not in the direction he pointed, he again nodded his head and spoke the words: "Over there."

I did as he said and saw, coming up the street, five figures dressed in black from hood to shoe. I didn't move, hoping that I would become one with the garbage pile and the wall. Across the street and twenty yards down, the figures stopped. Two of them began spray-painting the wall of a house while the others jogged in place, holding small hatchets in the air. I looked at the goat and he too was watching as the wall became a beach of white paint, and then a map of green with a blood-red hawk splitting the country in half. This is how, I thought, the walls of Jabaliya were painted. When the goat looked over at me, I am certain that he was half-smiling and thinking exactly the same thing.

With each passing night, the goat talked more and more. Still, most nights he grazed in silence as we discovered the stories of the curfew-enshrouded camp. We rarely saw the soldiers that I, and I am certain many others among the hundred thousand refugees in Jabaliya, thought were everywhere. These same soldiers who stalked our dreams and dared us to peek out our doors or tiny shuttered windows. In fact, in those first two weeks, I—we—saw soldiers only once, and that in passing. On several occasions, we had seen headlights skulking the streets of blocks five and six, but, although we'd assumed they were jeeps, they could as easily have been workers returning from their cheap-labor jobs in the orange fields and kitchens and butcher shops of the occupiers.

"Where are all the soldiers?" I asked the goat late one night, unusual for me; I usually listened.

The words dangled there for a while before the goat rose on his hind legs, pressing his front hooves against the graffiti-painted wall; each click they made along the cement raced through the encroaching dawn like gunfire. He chewed on a leaf from a locust tree, then another. More time passed before he turned to me and plainly uttered his answer to my question.

"They rule us by our imaginations."

"How do you mean?"

"Just look at you now. You are studying me standing here, thinking that I look like the soldiers have me against the wall, patting me down, checking my identification papers."

"So what if I am thinking that?"

"Where else, other than this place, would someone think of something as ridiculous as a goat being patted down by soldiers? How often all over the world are goats doing the same thing, just stretching for something to busy their mouths? And yet, even though you see exactly what I am doing, you don't pay attention to what you are seeing, but rather, you are imagining, crazy though it may be, what the army has seared into your mind."

I moved my eyes to the dust. The goat went back to picking at the leaves. If I'd had a watch I would have checked it and kept checking, counting the minutes until my work finished for the night and I could go home to where my wife was making fresh bread, which I would break and share with her before going off to my mat to sleep.

⌁

The nineteenth moon had abandoned Jabaliya and the night was cool, not cold, for mid-May. The air held in it the feel of rain, but the rainy season was seven months away.

That night the goat was acting a little strange, not his talkative self, and in the first hours of darkness we had only walked a short way from Ghassan's. In fact, we were only fifty yards from my house—so close that when I asked the goat if he was okay and he replied that he was feeling slightly chilled, I offered to get him a jacket.

"No, don't trouble yourself," he said.

To which I said, "Don't be ridiculous, the house is a minute away. Come on, you can meet my wife."

"I'll stay here and wait."

"Ghassan told me to never let you out of sight."

"It's fine. Like you said, the house is right over there."

With that I went up the street, but I looked back two or three times, feeling uncomfortable about leaving the goat alone, even for a short while. Once, he raised his leg in a wave, as if he were telling me not to worry. Before opening the door of my house, I looked yet again and the goat hadn't moved from where he stood. My wife gave me a surprised look when she saw me.

"I have only come for a jacket."

"Where's the goat?"

"Just outside."

"You told me you weren't supposed to leave him alone."

"He's cold. Do we have something he can wear?"

My wife went into the bedroom and came out with a jacket of our son's.

"This should fit him better than one of yours, although I have never clothed a goat before."

I wasn't certain if my wife was joking or not, so I thanked her and went back outside. Down the street, I saw nothing, but I wasn't too concerned. Each step I took, still unable to see the goat, increased my anxiety, so much so that halfway down School Street I began to run, cradling the jacket under my arm. I searched everywhere, saying nothing, for if the soldiers were in the area I didn't want to alert them in any way. Then I heard a haunting snicker coming from above. I forced my head toward the sound and saw the goat atop one of the houses.

Relieved that he was okay, I did not question how he came to be up there. I held out the jacket and the goat jumped from the ten-foot-high roof, landing gently on the street.

"Let me help you," I offered.

The goat lifted his front right hoof through the left sleeve, then the left hoof through the right, and I zipped the coat up his back, careful not to snag his fur. The sleeves were a bit loose, but the length nearly perfect and it fit snugly.

"Like it was made for you."

"Thank you," said the goat.

"Are you hungry?" I held out a piece of flatbread given to me by my wife.

"No, thank you. Let's rest, I feel tired."

I placed the piece of bread in the pocket of the goat's jacket. He led me in the direction of the market and when we drew close, he stopped.

"Why do we allow that tower to stand?"

I turned to the watchtower a hundred yards away.

"What do you propose we do?"

"I don't propose anything. But imagine how simply we as a group could bring it down. With all the people we have in the camp, we could…"

A beam from the large spotlight stabbed us from above. Blinded, I shielded my eyes with my arm. Soon the headlights from a jeep and then another found us.

"Don't move," shouted the soldiers, about thirty yards away. I obeyed them, but the goat moved away from me and closer to the wall.

"We said to stop!"

"Listen to them," I told the goat, but he acted as though he didn't hear.

"Not another step!"

"He's just a goat," I said.

"I don't care what he is."

"A simple goat; he can't understand you."

The soldiers edged closer. "What is he wearing?"

"A jacket," I answered. "He's cold."

"You just told me he's a goat. How the hell do you know he is cold?"

I almost said that the goat had told me, but I caught myself.

"I just know. It's my goat."

"Do you have a permit for the goat?"

"A permit?"

"You are not allowed to have any animal without a permit from the army."

"Goats need IDs?"

The goat took one step and then another toward the soldiers. Several shots were fired. The goat was thrown back ten feet before he hit the ground. He didn't move. The guns were trained on me.

"You. Go and remove the jacket from the goat. Slowly."

With guns raised, the soldiers began to back away from us. I went cautiously to the goat and knelt over him. I could see that he was dead.

"You sons of a whore. You killed the last goat from the village of al-Jiyya."

"Remove the jacket!"

Slowly, gently, I tried to unzip the coat, but the zipper caught and my shuddering hands could not release it.

"Take the jacket off!"

The blood of the goat had begun to pond in the street. I stared at it. Again, I worked on the zipper, and finally, it came free. I lifted the goat's left leg from a sleeve and began on the right. As I pushed the hoof up through the fabric, the leg broke cleanly in two. Sensing the soldiers about to open fire, I shoved the remainder of the leg through the sleeve and managed to remove the jacket. I held it up for the soldiers to see that there was nothing in it. No bomb. No weapon. Nothing other than a piece of flatbread, which fell to the street.

The soldiers drove away, leaving the both of us where they had found us. I didn't want to take the goat back to Ghassan immediately. Of course there was no traffic, so I didn't even bother to move him. Although we were near some houses, no one looked out their doors or windows.

I sat by the goat and didn't really think that much at all about how I would get him to his master's house, five minutes away. I didn't think about what Ghassan would say to me, the person he'd entrusted with the goat. Nor did it occur to me that I no longer had work and would soon return to chiseling away the hours of daytime just to get to the hours of sleep.

I picked up the severed right leg and studied the goat's hoof. Sturdy, yet delicate. I placed it atop the goat's body. Every once in a while, the beam of light from the watchtower passed; strangely, it didn't blind me as before, but somehow seemed now to be a part of me. The light stretched over and past us, across the blocks of six, seven, eight, and nine, and in the direction of the sea, then to the city three miles away, then to the south, and back into Jabaliya. Nothing else happened. My heart continued to knock on the closet of my chest and I listened to it. When I was a child, after playing soccer, I would stick my fingers in my ears and listen to the drumming of my heart. But I needed no fingers in my ears that night.

Like that I waited for the call to prayer, but it didn't come. Rather, from up the street, the clopping of a donkey cart could be heard and it became louder until it was upon me.

The man, whom I didn't recognize, spoke to me from the cart.

"What happened?"

"The soldiers killed Ghassan Abu Majed's goat."

He looked down at me, the night still slipping into dawn. I noticed for the first time that the man was hauling several dozen watermelons. He stepped down from the cart.

"Let me help you."

We placed the goat onto the back end of the cart.

"Is this Ghassan, the one from al-Jiyya?"

"Yes, he lives in block six."

I went back and picked up the jacket and thought that winter was such a long time away, and only the savage months of summer awaited.

—

I knew Ghassan would be up, for once he had told me he wakes at 4:30 exactly, sleeping away the entire curfew. That way he ignores it. My life, he told me, is fifteen-and-a-half-hour days.

Before the cart made it to Ghassan's house I saw him standing in the street and he came to meet us. He said nothing, barely gave me a glance, but went to the back of the cart, where he lifted the goat into his arms and carried him away.

I don't remember if I thanked the man with the cart or not. I cut through the alleyway and home. My wife said nothing as I walked inside; she may have sighed a sad sigh when I refused the food she offered, that I also do not remember.

~

I heard that Ghassan went to the field where the orange grove once stood and shoveled a grave. He dug and dug, refusing anyone's help, and while he dug no one left the field, in fact more and more people gathered.

Night had fallen when Ghassan finished digging. So deep was the hole that several men had to link themselves into a human rope in order to help Ghassan climb out.

Well into the incarceration of curfew, the procession left the field and passed through the camp. Everyone was certain that the soldiers were all places—in the alleys, on the rooftops, somehow a part of the graffiti on the walls, even in the willow tree. We could have told them differently, the goat and I, but who would have believed us?

~

No one saw Ghassan Abu Majed again. The morning after he buried his goat, Ghassan's wife checked the front room of the house, where he had been sleeping since their grandchild was born eight weeks before. When she didn't find her husband in the room, she thought nothing of it, believing he was at morning prayers.

She went outside and cleaned the clothes and the sun had begun to scorch them and still her husband had not returned. She asked passersby if they had seen him; all offered their condolences for the goat and added that, no, they had not seen Ghassan.

The heat of summer baked the streets of Jabaliya and dried the freshly washed black jeans of the youth within twenty minutes. Each afternoon at about three o'clock, the men of block six would take their chairs outside into the warm shade of the wall and they would whittle away the late afternoons as Ghassan had for decades. Here, the men talk and dream of the distant days of winter, and when winter comes they think of the days of summer while the rains keep them huddled inside their houses.

⌐

Half a year rushes past and it is the first day of winter's mist, and soon the mist will become droplets of rain and they will plink off the zinc-roofed houses.

My dream of the brittle days of summer is interrupted by a knocking, a tapping more like it, on the front door. I don't bother to move as I hear my wife walk by my room to the front of the house. She opens the metal door and its creaking reminds me of a job, long since promised and unfulfilled.

There are no voices and the door echoes its moan, shuts. And now there is a tapping on my room door.

"Yes."

The silhouette of my wife is there and it looks, in the low light, and through my squinted eyes, like another person as well. I say nothing, for my wife will certainly nag me about getting new glasses. When I sit up on the sleeping mat and look closer I see that she is holding a jacket.

"This was hanging on the door outside."

"Who was knocking?" I ask.

"There was no one there."

"Coats don't knock, my wife."

"There was no one there," she repeats.

I sigh as I get out from under the blanket.

"Hand me my sweater."

"Just put this on." She gives me the jacket.

I do as she says and the jacket is new and warm and it reminds me of my son. I shake off the ruthless thoughts of whether he too is warm on this December morning. Slipping into my sandals, I walk to the front of the house, and before opening the door I turn to my wife, who is right behind me.

"I will fix the door this afternoon."

She says nothing, and the sound as I open it mocks my procrastination. I look up and down the deserted, damp street and I am about to shut the door when I see the footprints facing me on the stoop.

"There was someone here," I say.

"Obviously, for the coat didn't arrive on its own."

I keep my attention on the ground. The top right corner of the right foot, where the last two toes should be, is missing. Ending at my door, the footprints then go in the opposite direction, back up the street.

Quickly I leave without telling my wife where I am going. Besides, I can hear her words, real or imagined, chasing me up the street. *Crazy man.* I wear the new jacket, the jacket for my son, following a long-missing man who believes he had a goat that could talk.

I remember what I once heard about Ghassan, many years before I met him. It is something of a legend, I guess, or used to be. As a young man, when he fled to Gaza in 1948, Ghassan carried his goat the entire nine miles, and when they arrived, he whispered a promise into its floppy ear.

Two years later, in 1950, the year the camp opened, Ghassan went out under the giant willow tree and, with a small hatchet, chopped the little toe from his right foot. The following year, on the same day, November 4th, he went to the willow once again and severed the next toe on his right foot. In 1952, the day before the anniversary, his wife-to-be approached him.

"And what are you going to do after eight years?" she asked.

"Take my fingers."

"And when they are gone?"

Ghassan said nothing and his wife-to-be jumped on the silence and answered her own question.

"If you want to marry me, you will raise the goats, as a memory of our village, and keep your toes."

And that is what happened—and why I am following, in light rain, the eight-toed footprints up the street. The farther I go, the more I am certain where they will lead me. I continue on, drawn by the inevitability of it all. Once I cross the rusted railroad tracks and enter the cemetery of the oranges, I am guided to a simple grave, a grave I have never visited but know for certain is the goat's.

The footprints end at the edge of the grave. I stare at them, hugging the warmth of the coat against my body. The drizzle patters off my head and my hair is wet before I realize that the jacket has a hood. I put it on and the rain patters against it, louder but more hollow. How hard must it fall, I wonder, before the footprints will be erased, or is it even possible that it will ever rain that hard again?

He marvels at, while at the same time is saddened by, how adept the children are at recognizing the sounds. How they tell him that the shot just heard was from a tear gas gun rather than a Kalashnikov or that was the sound of a bomb rather than an exploding Molotov cocktail. It is the children in the house who are the first to hear an army patrol wending its way up the night street. Or, at least, they are first to admit to hearing it.

~

The gurgle of falafel grease wakes him and he goes a couple of houses down the street. The morning already speaks of heat and he studies Aysa scooping ball after ball of the bright green chickpea batter into the pond of grease, watches them dance and brown and crisp.

In a short while, Aysa's little sister steps outside and sees the American and then disappears into an alleyway; before the falafel are cool enough to bite into, a half dozen children are there. Several of them exchange a coin for some breakfast falafel, others just come to watch the stranger, who has now become a familiar sight in the morning and early evening streets. Aysa hands him a falafel and, as always, refuses the coin.

~

Some take lemons each day, others a small bottle of cheap cologne and a rag, the grandmother, Fatima, hands the American half an onion to help combat the scorch of the tear gas.

~

He loves the nights, rare that they are, when he, and a few others, slip on black jackets and vanish into the lightless camp. They avoid the main streets and keep tight to either side of the alleyway walls, straddling the trough of open sewage. Once in a while they pass someone and whispered greetings are exchanged, as well as whether or not any soldiers have been seen.

One night, as they near their house in block number four, a jeep can be heard, and it is not far away. Then the beam of a spotlight startles the main street; the men separate and find different places along the alley walls, getting as close as possible. With his face against the cement blocks, he feels the geography of their pockmarks, and how, as if in defiance of curfew, they have held the sun's warmth in them. As the searchlight stalks the streets and the patrol passes, he draws even closer to the wall, realizing that it is here, and only here, where one can find a moment of solitude in this place.

—

A Three Cigarette Story

Once there was a beautiful and powerful hawk. It spent its days soaring high above the land and from so far up it could see everything that moved on the landscape below. The swiftest of rabbits, snakes, field mice. The hawk, when it saw something that it liked, would follow it from above and when the creature broke out into an open space the hawk would dive toward it with blinding speed. In flight it could adjust its speed and direction with a tilt of its wing. Nothing escaped the eyes of the hawk, nor, once the creature was in its claws, could it ever wriggle free.

One day, while in its nest, a large net was cast over the hawk and it was taken away. It fought and clawed and tried ripping the net with its powerful beak, but it couldn't break free. Soon the hawk found itself in a metal cage, the bars so close together that it could barely work its claws between them. The hawk couldn't spread its wings inside the cage and as the days passed into weeks its wings became useless. Unable to open its wings, they became bent and slowly the beautiful brown feathers began to fall and drift through the bars of the cage and float to the floor. After weeks of captivity became seasons the hawk was scrawny, ridiculous looking with its bowed wings and without feathers.

Suddenly, on a late winter's afternoon, the cage was opened and the hawk was free to go. The hawk took its time, looking all around for those who had captured him. The hawk waited and waited and when he saw no one, stepped cautiously to the edge of the cage, then took the final step and was in midair. Trying to spread its wings, the hawk couldn't do it; they remained bowed and the hawk plummeted to the floor, falling hard.

Stunned, the hawk looked up and saw the bottom of the swaying cage. He wondered how he would be able to get back inside. Knowing that it couldn't make it back to the cage by itself, the hawk began to screech, and even its screech had changed; it had lost all of its power for it had rarely done so in its captivity.

In time, one of the captors appeared and began mocking the hawk. He laughed and laughed before asking if he had had enough and would he like for him to help the hawk back into the cage. The hawk said yes, yes he would like help. The captor picked up the hawk and placed him into the cage. As he was about to shut the cage's door, the captor decided against it, for he knew that the hawk could not go anywhere without his help.

The cage door remained open and the hawk remained inside. Many cycles of the moon passed before the useless wings of the hawk fell off and then it was some time before its claws too were shed and stronger legs began to form. The hawk didn't know what was happening; for a long time he was frightened by this changing of himself.

Whenever the captors came to the cage, although it was rare that they did, the hawk cowered in the back corner, cowered under his fallen wings. When he was once again alone, the hawk marveled at his transformation. Legs nothing like a hawk's, arms grown in place of his wings, even his beak had been blunted. The hawk waited for his captors to come back and on the day that they did he was huddled in the corner as usual, but as soon as they turned their backs on him he leapt out of the open cage, pounced on the both of them, crushing them with his all-powerful arms.

The hawk rushed out of the building where he had spent so many years of his life and he ran and ran until he came to the tree where he nested and from where he was taken by the captors. He called up to the nest, which was smaller than he remembered. None of the hawks responded and so he called again and it was a while before one of the hawks peeked out of the nest and looked down upon him.

"What is it you want?" the bird in the nest asked.

"Don't you know me? It's me, your brother."

"My brother has been gone for years." The hawk pulled its head back into the nest and couldn't be seen.

"But it's me. I may not look the same, but it is true. Ask me a question; a question that only your brother would know the answer to."

The head of the hawk reappeared from the nest.

"What part of the rabbit do I like to eat first?"

"That's easy. The rear legs. You always eat the rear legs first."

Still doubting that it was his brother, the hawk asked a second question.

"What is my favorite kind of cloud?"

"That's easy too. You don't like clouds, for when hunting you can hide in them, but you always enjoyed the challenge of the hunt and never liked to hide in waiting."

The hawk in the nest was shocked and filled with joy and although he didn't recognize his brother he left the nest, landing softly on his brother's strong arms. The brother embraced the hawk and made as if he were going to kiss him, but instead, took his brother's neck in his hands and snapped it with a quick twist. He dropped his brother-hawk on the ground and walked back to the cage, which still had its door open, awaiting him.

—

Even here in Jabaliya, a place only rumored to have seen snow, the cold of Ohio stalks him.

⁓

The quarter-sized flakes batter the March landscape, the car being towed away during the late-night blizzard, the almost serene beauty of the snow pelting through the flashing yellow lights of the tow truck, growing smaller, dimmer until gone.

Snow continues to fall and twelve nights later the throttling ring of the phone and now it is his father who has been taken from him. A year before, nearly to the day, he cried while standing over the open casket of his father's father, fingering rosary beads as the priest plowed through the prayers.

Now he stands above his father's casket, minus the rosary beads, and thinks of the dwindling number of men in the family and of himself and how he made the two-hundred-mile trip in a borrowed car—his perfectly ironed shirts, done with care by a friend an hour after the phone call, flapping in the breeze of the rolled down window. And he walks up the fifteen steps, following the pall bearers into the church and then to the cemetery he goes across the still-frozen ground in shoes, like the car, not even his own, and he places a rose, red, and feels his lips against the second of April, cold-skinned casket.

⁓

That afternoon, following the funeral, he and his friends from Ohio walk past the house where he grew up, but was sold several years before. He looks over the stone wall into the backyard where he once played baseball and football alone for hours. Back then, he could never see over the wall, but now it seems so much lower and the yard so much smaller. His friend, who loaned him the car, comments on how he would love to go into the house and look around. They don't. He can't wait to get back in his borrowed car and drive west once again.

⟋

The quiet, more than the God, is what he seeks in the church. Each morning he goes to the earliest Mass. A gather of old men and women speckle the spacious pews. He is careful, when kneeling, to hide the bottoms of his shoes so that the woman, two pews back, doesn't see the holes in them. He responds to the prompts of the priest, takes the Eucharist into his hollow stomach and returns to the pew, the same one every morning, and he wishes to lie down on the soft wood and pillow his head on the hymnals and sleep the mornings and days and nights and ache away.

⟋

When he is able to get a car, he goes into the city and begins to meet some of the homeless. One day in the city library he meets a homeless man from Alabama. They talk of the difficulties in going back home and asking for help. The two of them go that evening to a church basement and get a meal. He pretends that he, too, is homeless, but they all know he is not.

⟋

Through a patch of woods, five minutes from the house, there is a one room library. He goes there during the days to escape the chill of the house, the loneliness, the knocks on the door, the pestering of the phone. He has never read literature before, only magazines and a lot of newspapers. The librarian leaves him alone, as if she knows.

He begins with the smallest of the books—works by Wilder and Steinbeck and Orwell—and they blanket his coldness, people his loneliness, muffle the knuckles against the door and the gnawing whispers in his mind. This becomes his new church, a place where god answers his prayers.

⟋

The Boy Who Sold Martyrs

A man once asked me:
   "Do birds cry?"
   To which, I replied:
   "Just listen."

If you are fortunate enough to live in one of the houses in Jabaliya camp across the street from the giant willow, then you are blessed by its cooling shade from the early afternoon summer sun and, in winter, if the winds are blowing from the southeast, as they so often do, then the tree serves as a buffer of sorts from the chilled rains.

In one of these houses, the house with the blue door, stands a boy in the back room staring at the martyrs lying, side by side, on the sleeping mat.

The boy is in his early teens, as easily thirteen as fifteen. Looking down at him from above—in the eight-inch gap between the rusty metal roof and the cement block wall—one can see the bald patch on the top right side of his head, a red-brown island of skin amidst the boy's muddled soot-black hair, a scar from a spill of hot oil when he was two. The boy is tall for his age, but thin, and when he walks one can see that he has yet to grow into his body; he lopes and his gangly legs bump, at times, into the cart that he pushes to and from the market each day.

One by one the boy looks at each of the photos of the martyrs arranged by the date of their deaths. Each evening, before going to sleep, he arranges the pictures in a different way: by block numbers, by whether they smiled in their final photo or not, by the place they died. He picks up one of the photos and says the martyr's name, pausing five seconds before placing it atop the small cart sitting in the room.

He repeats this for each of the fourteen martyrs, then, when all the pictures are atop the cart, the boy closes his eyes for an extended period of time.

In addition to being able to see many things more than most observers, and from vantage points beyond their capabilities, I can also read the boy's mind; right now, for instance, the boy, with his eyes closed, is imagining the latest martyr and what she, yes she, looks like. The first female martyr in Gaza.

The thin, whip-like branches of the willow are not conducive to nesting. Not that it affects me in any real way, since I am a pigeon who likes to roost—roosting is much less permanent than nesting. Still, the willow offers a rare high vantage point looking over the cement forest of Jabaliya. Because of my habit of roosting, this is how I first learned of the boy, the seller of martyrs, whose name is Ahmed.

It was a brutally hot afternoon, the kind of day where the heat presses a bird closer to the ground to the point of where you feel as though you are not flying at all. I was exhausted, seeking shade where I could rest, but not wanting to fly the three miles into Gaza City where the higher buildings cast longer shadows. Shade is a rarity in Jabaliya.

About two o'clock I saw that the shadow of the willow had begun to stretch across School Street and onto the houses that sidled it. I landed on house number twenty-eight, the only one in the shade with a light blue door, my favorite color. The roof was also without much of the clutter that covers most of the houses, namely TV antennas, chunks of wood and branches, water tanks, and, every once in a while, a plastic chair or two. I perched in the shaded area of the roof and, tired that I was, stayed there dozing on and off while the blur of the street passed. It so happened that I was still there on the front part of the roof when the boy came home, pushing the cart inside.

He looked up at me, I, down at him, and that was it until a while later when he came back out with a handful of crumbled bread and tossed it up to me. From the first, I liked the boy. By the simple act of throwing the bread up to me, rather than on the ground where I would have had to go and get it, I knew he had a warm heart or, at least, the possibilities of one. The bread scattered on the roof and I ate it leisurely.

It continued like this for many afternoons and, in time, I began to roost at night on the spot at the back of the house, where I am this morning watching the boy prepare his cart for a day of work.

Ahmed has finished packing the cart and takes it out of the room and to the front of the house. He kisses his mother good morning and they share a small bowl of scrambled eggs and warm flatbread. I know that later, after the boy is finished with work, whatever remains of the bread will be mine.

⟋

At the risk of sounding conceited, and there is nothing worse than a conceited bird, I am no ordinary pigeon. I come from a lineage of pigeons, the great carrier pigeons of the early twentieth century, birds that transported messages from country to country, war zone to war zone, saving many soldiers and civilians alike. We are also known for our superior vision.

In the language of the people of Jabaliya, we are called *zajil,* a kind of storyteller, if you will. Not all of us can see into the minds of humans. In fact, few of us can. My father, for example, could not do so, but both my grandfather and grandmother could. Anyway, all that I am trying to say is that it is natural for me to be interested in stories. After Ahmed began to toss me the breadcrumbs, it is his story that I became interested in, and through observing him for the past year I have begun to piece together his life.

⟋

It was not the day, that rainy February morning when his father's body was found washed ashore, after he fell overboard from his fishing boat, that the boy began thinking of selling photos of the dead. Nor was it when the boy's uncles and neighbors tried holding him back from seeing the bloated corpse; in those days the boy still could clearly remember his father's features. As the funeral procession made its way to the other end of the camp, he easily pictured his father's prominent jawline and the ears which had a slight bow to them. The rain clutched the red, black and green flag to the coffin and the boy believed that the clouds also mourned his father, a thought that comforted him.

Months later, the final week of elementary school, the boy was shocked that he couldn't remember his father's features. Ears, mouth, nose, eyes, all of them disappeared leaving only a blank, very white face with the brownish red hair atop it. During the middle of math class, the boy ran out of the school, across the playground, and home. He buried his tears in his mother's collarbone and when he was able to manage the words he asked:

"Do we have any photos of Father?"

She was silent in her thoughts and answered him in a befuddled tone.

"No, I don't think so."

After a week of inquiring with family members she gave her son a definitive that there was not a single photo to be found.

"Just close your eyes and remember a good time with him and you can picture your father," she said one evening that summer.

"I've tried, but his face is blank."

"Try drawing a picture of him."

"I have, but it never comes out like Father."

"Try again."

The next day, as the boy was playing soccer, a funeral procession stopped the game and Ahmed watched as they carried the wooden coffin down the street, not to the cemetery where his father was buried, but to the Martyrs' Cemetery between blocks six and seven. It was a long procession, so much longer than when his father died, so long that the boy's sweat had dried to a salty film by the time it passed. He saw many of the mourners carrying photos of the dead man and the boy thought, unlike him, they would never forget what the man looked like.

⁓

The following month, in January, 2004, the first suicide bomber in Gaza killed himself and eleven others on a bus in Jerusalem. I remember this day vividly for I had flown to the desert, a place I like to sometimes go when the humidity of the coast becomes too much. I find myself, as

I grow older, and we pigeons do not live all that long, with more and more of an urgency to get away from this Gaza. Once, last winter, I started to fly westward and for two and a half days I continued on, slowly making my way across the Sinai all the way to the great city of Cairo where I nibbled from crumbs of sesame bread at Tahir Square and was fed the finest *halva* paste from a kindly old woman along the banks of the Nile.

That day I am talking about, the day of the first suicide bomber from Gaza, I had spent an afternoon and a night in the desert and had had my fill of it and was happy to be going home. As the center of Gaza City came into view, and off in the distance the Sea, a missile roared past, so close that the wave of heat from it knocked me back and scorched my left wing, which still, to this day, bears the rough, hardened edges on my carpal.

Before I regained my senses, an explosion rocked the city. I did not know where to go. I thought of retreating to the desert, but decided on the beach where I found a tangle of brambles and stayed the night there while the explosions blistered the city and camps.

Funerals jammed the streets over the next days and I watched them from above, although my injured left wing made it painful to fly. Luckily, there was a nice wind where I could soar for the most part; only when landing or taking off did the pain raise tears in my red-black eyes.

Back in Jabaliya, the boy followed in several of the funeral processions and was enamored by the photos of the dead. There were so many photos and he wondered where they could have all come from so quickly, within hours of their deaths. Some of the photos were large, pasted on a board and carried above the heads of the mourners; others fit neatly into one's pocket. The smaller pictures were what the boy liked the most, easy to take with you and look at whenever and wherever one had the desire to be reminded of the dead person. But still, the unanswerable question: How could these photos be made so quickly? Only from God could they come.

Ahmed continued to follow along in the processions of the martyrs, which often quickly turned into protests against the former occupiers, who now, rather than being a daily presence in the Gaza Strip, strike at the camps and cities from helicopters and jets and tanks and sometimes the military enters the Strip before pulling back within a few days.

After the funerals, there is a week of mourning and Ahmed goes to the houses of the dead and drinks the bitter black coffee, which he likes, and eats the sweet dates, which he doesn't like. Sometimes he is given a photo of the martyr and he has begun to collect them and soon he has eight. Most of the pictures are in black and white; a couple, however, are in color.

One day while in the market, Ahmed was fascinated by an old man selling relics of the occupation: bullet casings, tear gas canisters marked *Made in the USA,* necklaces with rubber bullets, shreds of army uniforms. He asked the man if he had any photos to sell.

"Photos of what?"

"Of those who died at the hands of the soldiers, or the suicide bombers."

The old man rubbed his gray beard.

"That's a good idea, young man. Why don't you do that?"

"I'm not really sure how to do it."

"Just sell them. What needs to be done?"

The boy rushed home and took out the photos he had collected and placed in a special yellow envelope. He told his mother about what the old man said and she thought that it wasn't a bad idea, if for no other reason than to keep her son busy during the weeks of summer vacation. That evening the boy's mother took a piece of rope, which she used for hanging laundry, nailed the ends to two pieces of wood, tall as the boy, and with clothespins pinched each of the photos onto the rope. She told her son to take it to the market the next day.

"But what if I sell one of the pictures?"

"Isn't that what you want to do?"

"I only have one of each."

"Make copies of the photos."

"But where?"

"Find out."

The next afternoon Ahmed took the photos to Gaza City where he met Salim, the man everyone advised him to go see. Inside the shop sat a large machine, a copier, he told Ahmed, and it was with this that he could make prints of the pictures. He gazed admiringly at the machine. So this, he thought, was the God from where the photos were born.

"How much are the pictures?"

Salim quoted the price; reading the face of the boy, he asked:

"What are you planning to do with them?"

The boy told him and, like the old man the day before, he too liked the idea.

"Tell you what, I will make you two copies of each photo at no cost and when you sell them you can pay me, plus an additional ten percent."

Ahmed returned to Jabaliya with the photos and began selling them the next morning.

⚊

The greatest thing about being a bird is that we have no borders. During the occupation, I flew near and above the long lines at the checkpoints, above the thousands of workers waiting to cross the Green Line to their low-paying, labor-intensive jobs. No hands ever rummaged over my body, patting me down, never checked my ID card, never turned me back at the border and sent me home without explanation.

Many times I go to the former villages and towns of pre-1948 Palestine. I have flown over and landed upon remnants of crumbled stone houses, waterless wells, and weed sprouting walls. I have seen fields misted by sprinklers in the early morning; through this water I have flown and cooled off in its spray.

These are the haunted places that I hear spoken of in the low light of the nights in the camps. Burayr. Hamama. Hatta. Kawkaba. Najd. On days after visiting these places, I am saddened and wish that I could write, on a piece of paper, simple sentences that these places exist only in the memory, and like memories the truth and reality of it is stretched, molded, reformed, and sometimes forgotten altogether. If I could, I would write my simple sentences, roll them up on a simple piece of paper, tie it around my simple neck and, like my ancestors, deliver the news to those who have not lived in those villages and towns for more than half a century.

Most, I believe, know of the fate of their villages, but they still tell the stories to their children and grandchildren. What else are they to do with the threads of stories and memories—swallow and allow them to lacerate their tongues and throats, carrying them unspoken to their muted graves?

⁓

Young men give up their lives, often taking others with them, and Ahmed goes to the funerals seeking photos of the brothers, husbands, sons, grandsons. But today is different. This morning, as I see him take his cart down the street and to the market, he will work only until lunch because, after noon prayers, the funeral for the first female suicide bomber will be held in block number eleven.

I fly above Ahmed, down the street for a short while, before turning off toward the sea, where I will clean up and then, like many in Jabaliya, I will also attend the funeral.

⁓

The swell of mourners begins early in the north end of the camp and stretches to where the railroad once passed. For such a large mass of people there is only a hum rising, like the dust in June, ankle-high. I settle atop a roof across the street from the dead woman's house. An old man throws several crumbs below me, a foot and a foot and another foot apart, as though he is trying to snare me. It wouldn't be the first time that someone has tried such a thing. I ignore him.

Ahmed is late in coming, held up by a last-minute buyer. By the time he is halfway up the street, the door to the woman's house has flung open, the remains of the body in its eternal bed and the once quiet crowd has grown to a fury of chants. The boy moves to the side then climbs his way onto a roof. I fly down to where he is and land five feet away, separated only by the width of the alleyway. He looks over at me, but quickly turns to the stream-like flow of the crowd below.

As the procession passes, the coffin is in the middle of it like a lone ship at sea. I notice, as does the boy, that there are no photos being carried. Like I, he can only imagine what she looks like and wonder: if he has ever seen her, has she ever bought a photo from him, did she smile into the camera, if there ever was a camera to smile into. When the coffin is by us the boy sees it, a photo, smaller, like the ones he sells. But from up here he cannot see it clearly. He jumps into the alleyway and joins in the river of people trying to inch his way closer to the only photo of the woman.

⁓

Her photo is taped on the coffin. The boy, unable to get near the grave, again climbs onto a roof, in time to see the coffin lowered into the hole by a hundred hands. He sees what he believes to be the mother and is astonished by her face and the lack of tears trundling down her cheeks, the nonexistent wails of grief from her mouth.

Why isn't she crying, he wonders. He thinks back to his father's funeral and doesn't recall himself crying either. Only before and after did he cry, almost always in the morning when, at breakfast, the absence of the sparkling flakes of sardines, always found in his father's hair in the morning, were no longer there. It was this that made him most sad.

Maybe this is why, he thinks, they bury the photo with the coffin; some people, perhaps, just don't want to remember.

I watch the boy and want to go over and rest on his shoulder and deliver to him a scrawled message, which I would carry around my neck. This time, if only I could, I would write: for some the grief is so powerful that any reminder of their loved one would crumble them, the living, to a powder, a powder so fine it can be carried like the *khamaseen* winds each spring carry the flour-like sand for thousands of miles, so far away from the one they want most to remain closest to.

⁓

On my trip to Cairo, and in other places I have ventured, I have seen groups of pigeons flying together, sometimes dozens of them, and they return to the same rooftop from where they began. Recently I have begun to see them more and more in Gaza as well. I have mixed emotions about these distant kin of mine; on the one hand I am a little envious how they always have a place to go home to and food to eat.

That is also the reason I do not envy them, the simple fact that they cannot just go off to anyplace they want. I am not sure if they could even do this, even if they wanted to, given the way they have been trained. I have heard that these pigeons live two or sometimes three times longer than I, a pigeon in the wild.

But what if one of those birds wanted to fly off in the middle of the night, just like that, and follow a young boy from his house to the Martyrs' Cemetery? What if they wanted to watch, from a gravestone, the boy jab the shovel into the soil? And would those pigeons try to warn the boy of what he is about to do? Or, like me, remain a silent witness?

～

The soil has yet to turn to the color of dust, the night keeping it soft and easy for the boy to dig. The repetition and his tired muscles give him a distraction from what he is doing. When a car approaches, the boy goes flat to the ground and waits for the lights and groan of the engine to disappear. When it does, he returns to the digging and soon the shovel knocks on the coffin. This is the worst moment of the night. Every time the shovel hits the coffin, the boy is certain that it knocks back at him. He knows that it can't be true, but can't stop himself from believing that it is. He leans over and reaches into the grave and clears away, with his blistered hands, the dirt, until he feels the picture. A beating of the female martyr's heart thrums in his fingertips, through his dirt-encrusted nails. He stops, takes his hands off the coffin, only then realizing that it is the sprint of his heart that he feels gnawing his fingertips.

He forces himself back to the coffin and slowly removes the picture. The darkness is such that he can't see the picture and he places it in the envelope that he has brought and quickly refills the hole, smoothing the dirt as best he can. He moves the dirt with his sandals, erasing most of his footprints.

I am about to leave the gravestone from where I have been watching, but stay behind and let the boy make his way home alone.

～

Early the next morning, when the light is enough for the boy to see the picture, he puts it on his sleeping mat and studies it. The face of the woman is soiled with splotches of dirt; dirt is stuck to the eyes, most of the mouth and much of her headscarf. Some of the dirt he is able to scratch away with his fingernail, but much of it, the bottom layer, when he tries to remove it, part of the picture, a small blemish on the right side of her face, tears off. Afraid he will damage more of the photo, he places it reverently on his pillow and again studies it. When his mother knocks on the door, the boy covers the picture with a sheet.

"Are you okay? Breakfast is ready."

"I'm feeling a little sick. I'll go to work in the afternoon."

"Do you need some medicine?"

"No, I'll just sleep a little."

He waits until he hears his mother open the front door, probably to do laundry, and then uncovers the photo. If only he could clean the mouth area, he thinks, just enough to see if she is smiling. Or her eyes even, that would tell me a lot about her. He opens the door a crack, and seeing no one, hurries toward his mother's room. On the shelf he grabs a small bottle of rubbing alcohol, takes a hand towel from the kitchen and when he turns, standing there is his mother.

"How did you get so filthy?"

He looks at his hands and shirt and slacks for the first time in the brighter light at the front of the house.

"I was cleaning the cart."

"In your room?"

"I will take it outside."

"I thought you were sick?"

"More tired than sick. I couldn't sleep last night so I started to clean the cart early this morning. I didn't take it outside because I thought I would wake you."

He checks the dirt under his nails and thinks, not of the grave, although that is pecking away at his thoughts, but of the lie he told his mother. Both, he is aghast at, but perhaps even more so the lie.

His mother places her forehead against his, feeling for a fever, and he freezes, thinking that she can certainly read his lie. She pulls back and carefully looks at him.

"What happened to your hand and arms?"

"I told you I was cleaning the cart."

"What are these cuts from?"

The boy moves away from his mother and goes to his room.

"Ahmed, what is going on?"

He comes out with his envelope of pictures, added to it, the stolen photo.

"I have to get more prints made."

"What about breakfast? How about telling me what is going on?"

"I have to go to the city. I'll be home as soon as I finish."

Walking down the street, the boy is certain everyone knows what he did. He ignores them and walks faster, cutting through the school grounds and out back through the cactus field, which he hates to go through, but is also a shortcut. I follow him. In the field he sits down and removes the towel and rubbing alcohol, which he placed in his jacket. He dabs some of the alcohol onto the towel and gently touches the dirt-covered eyes of the female martyr.

He thinks, at first, that it is working, but by the time he has cleaned the eyes he sees that the alcohol has removed the eyes altogether, leaving only a crooked white smudge where the eyes used to be. Like acid, like magic. The boy embraces the photo and begins to cry.

"I'm sorry. I'm sorry." He rocks back and forth as though comforting an infant. At arm's length he holds the picture, trembling, chilled. I am watching from one of the cactuses, careful of the hair-like thorns. I see the boy deteriorate, like the woman's eyes in the photo. I turn away, but can't help myself, and I look at the boy, through embarrassed eyes, once again. Sometimes, reading minds is a curse.

Suddenly, the boy stands up and spins around looking at all the cactuses. Many of them look like people, one of the main reasons he doesn't like coming here. He begins to race through the field, away from the camp and he doesn't stop until, gasping for breath, he comes to the dirt road in back of the field. He allows himself time to recover. When he does, he continues at a slow, but steady, pace. Knowing where he is going, I fly up ahead and wait for him to arrive.

⌐

That he doesn't know what the woman looks like maddens the boy. How can he categorize her without knowing whether she smiled or not, or how her eyes stared into or averted the camera. It is only by the photos that he can in any way try to attempt to understand what they were thinking in those hours or days before they left Jabaliya for the final time. Did they too feel the things he sometimes felt? Frustration, loneliness, the scorching need to escape this place, and even those moments of excitement, like when he sells a photo or two.

He arrives at the shop looking as if he has been crying again. His hair is befuddled like an abandoned nest, his glazed dark eyes are distant and bruised with sadness. He does nothing to hide the fact that he has been crying. He walks into the shop and Salim is cropping a photo.

"Hi, Ahmed..." He pauses, then goes over to the boy. "Are you okay?"

"Can you bring back her eyes?" The boy begins to sob, but manages the words.

With a puzzled look, Salim takes the picture.

"Where did you get this?"

"At the funeral. I dropped it in the mud and tried cleaning it with alcohol."

"It's impossible to bring back the eyes."

"How about cleaning the dirt from the rest of the face?"

"I can try that, but I don't think it will turn out very well."

Salim takes the picture and makes a copy. The eyes and the smudges from the dirt look even worse.

"I also went to the funeral, but I saw no pictures."

"There were only a couple and one of them was dropped. I picked it up."

The boy becomes agitated and fumbles with the envelope of the photos.

"I need some extra prints of each of these pictures."

Salim, still holding the photo, gives the boy a concerned look.

"Are you sure that you're okay?"

"It's just that I will never know what she looks like." He points to the picture in Salim's hand.

"Why must you know what they look like?"

"So I don't forget their faces, like I have forgotten my father's."

Salim says nothing, glancing away from the boy's face. He takes the envelope and goes to the machine and makes two copies of each, including that of the female martyr.

⟋

Before returning to Jabaliya, the boy goes down Omar El Muhktar Street and to the beach. The night before, while on his way to the cemetery, he had made a promise to himself, something to make up for what he was about to do.

He sits in the sand and watches the waves crash and race up the shore then retreat. The repetition helps to calm him. Over and over, steady, certain. A woman catches his eye. At first he thinks she is playing with a child, making a castle in the sand. As he watches, he sees no one else with her. He moves closer and studies the drawing she is making on the beach. She looks up. She is beautiful.

"What are you doing?" he asks.

"I'm making a map."

He studies the map, but isn't sure what to make of it.

"Go up there, atop the mound, and it will be easier to see."

He does and it is clear from there what she is drawing. The map every child is taught at home, the map that is seared into their minds at school. It is large, two or three times larger than the boy. He watches her from the mound and when she finishes, she asks:

"Can you see it?"

"Yes, clearly. It's wonderful."

"Thank you."

And like that she walks away, southward along the beach. Ahmed watches until she is a mere dot and then he goes to the map in the sand, careful not to step on the borders. As she was finishing the map, the idea came to him that this is the perfect spot to fulfill his promise of the night before while in the cemetery.

With his hands he makes fifteen holes inside the map and buries a martyr in each of them. His promise, his penance; give the martyrs another place, a more beautiful resting place than in Jabaliya.

⟋

A week passes and the boy must make several trips to the city to keep up with the demand. Each time he orders more prints, he stops by the beach and buries one. He has sold more than forty of them during the week of mourning—the foggy-like quality of the photo, the eyeless stare mesmerizing you. I have, myself, been entranced by the picture, at times unsettling while at others a drug-like tonic dragging you into its comforting depths. I find myself gazing at the photo, which the boy has taped on the wall of the house, right next to the door of his room, perhaps specifically in order for me to see. There have been times when I have been so mesmerized by the photo that long stretches of time have gone by.

After the week of mourning, the boy is in his normal place in the market, talking to a customer, when a woman walks by, slowing down and looking at the photos. She passes back and forth numerous times and each time that she does she gets closer to the cart.

Then she stops, two steps from the boy. The woman takes those two steps and with one sweep of the hand has the photos—all fifteen martyrs—in her grasp and she is tearing them to pieces. She throws the fragments into the air and they flutter in all directions, somersaulting onto the vendors and their goods—tomatoes, cucumbers, apples, into bubbling *falafel* grease, onto the boy himself.

"Just like their lives," the woman shouts. "A thousand pieces, never whole again."

⌐

The boy finds out that the woman is the mother of the girl in the picture. In the coming days, he discovers the first female martyr was eighteen years old and a first-year university student. For many days the boy stays in the house, telling his mother that he is sick, but she knows the truth, heard about it the very evening it happened from many who witnessed it, and some who didn't.

It is at this time that the boy stops feeding me and I begin to find other places in Jabaliya to roost. Some nights I leave the camp altogether and spend it in the city or one of the other seven camps in the Gaza Strip. I find myself antsy, however, and after a night or two away I return to Jabaliya, sometimes even to the boy's house.

On one such morning, a couple of weeks later, the boy opens his bedroom door and I am shocked by his gauntness. He hugs and kisses his mother and eats a little breakfast then tells her he is going to the city. She is relieved that he has eaten something and is leaving the house for the first time in a long while.

He takes the back of a donkey cart most of the way and walks the rest. Walking, he looks even more awkward in all his thinness. Surprising me, he doesn't go to Salim's, but stops at a bakery where he buys a piece of sweet honey pastry. When the vendor cuts a square of the pastry, the bees hover above it only to return when the vendor goes away.

The boy takes small bites of the pastry and then looks up at me sitting on a street sign. I think he is going to offer me the last piece, which I usually don't like because of its sweetness, but so overjoyed that he is paying me a little attention I would gladly fly down and gorge myself on it, if offered, not caring that it would make me sick for days. I lift my wings a little, but realize that the boy is not looking at me, but through me; he doesn't notice me at all. He throws the remainder of the pastry into a side street. A couple of pigeons swoop down and fight over it and I watch until one gives up and flies away, leaving the pastry for the other to slowly peck away at.

⁓

I do not follow the boy to the photo shop, but watch from the street sign, a block away. He is inside for about fifteen minutes and I see him come out with a yellow envelope in hand, the same as the one within which he keeps the photos. He appears happy and the feeling of elation that coursed through me minutes ago, when I thought he noticed me, returns. The boy heads toward the beach and I wait until he is nearly out of sight before lifting off from the street sign and trailing him.

I land on the knoll of grassy sand, the same from which the boy watched the woman draw the map on the beach. The map, of course, has long since been washed away, but the boy knows the place of his private cemetery. I observe him digging a hole and, as he always does, he says a small prayer in a whisper, before covering the photo with sand. The boy closes the envelope, and when he turns his back on the waves, meets my eyes and holds them for a fleeting moment. He walks northward along the beach, in the direction of Jabaliya. I linger on the knoll, content and certain that he recognized me.

⌇

I lie on the knoll of sand, perhaps I have even allowed myself to slip into the bliss of a quick nap. Refreshed, I scamper and begin to claw away at the sand; never have I been much with my claws, nothing like a hawk or other bird of prey. I tire easily and stop often.

The sun has extinguished itself in the sea, pulling the half-moon into the apex of the sky. The light is ample for me to work by. On and off I dig; there is no rush.

By morning, the fishermen have finished their nights of work and head home to sleep, their skin and hair sparkle with the silver flakes of sardines, like that of the boy's father used to do. Rising hot, the sun grows hotter. It is midday before my claw scratches the picture. Faster I dig until the photo reveals itself. Exhausted though I am, I coax my wings up and down, up and down until I am above the city and pointed in the direction of the camp.

⌇

Within twenty minutes I am in Jabaliya on my familiar perch at the back of the boy's house. The boy's door is closed, but the yellow envelope is sitting on the small table along with some flatbread, the crumbs of which tease my longing stomach. I have never flown into the house; where I sit now is the closest I have been. But the bread crumbs are too much for me and I swoop down and onto the table. Piece by piece I devour the crumbs.

Engrossed in my hunger, I do not hear the unlocking of the front door and the boy's mother is near the table before I react. I take off, dropping the bread from my mouth. In a panic I fly in the wrong direction where there is no way out. I circle, trying to get my bearings, but it is as though I am in a maze in this house I am so familiar with. Before

I find my way to the back of the house, my escape, I see the boy's mother opening the yellow envelope and I hear the noose of grief trapped in her throat, strangling her.

⌁

Have you ever seen a bird cry? That question asked of me a while ago.

Maybe you think that we can't or don't or simply refuse to. But, just close your eyes for a minute and think back to when you have seen a mother bird feed her babies and remember the care and love that goes into it. Or, think of how we build our nests with so much pride, or, for that matter, how we protect, in any way we can, our unhatched eggs.

To you doubters, I say, anything that can love, can cry.

⌁

The boy's mother keeps her son's photo in the envelope. Only when alone, in the early morning while eating the fresh, warm bread, does she sometimes take out the picture and embrace it with her longing eyes. On these mornings, after we share our tears, she leaves behind a piece of the bread for me, and next to it, sitting on the table, is the photo of the boy for me to see.

On days when he doesn't have a ride into town, he takes the battered bicycle six miles to the woodshop. Most days he is alone and he loves the feel of the saw and the moan of the wood and knowing that he has plunged to the deepest of the well; some days, slivers of light can be seen peeking through the darkness.

⟋

Days that he brings the bicycle, winter or spring, he doesn't bother sweeping off the beard of sawdust, allowing the wind against his face to peel it from him, scattering something of himself across the Ohio landscape.

⟋

One year later, in November, he moves to the nation's capital, spending his first nights in the back of a rusted Chevette. With him, a box of books, and each night in the car he takes them out and opens them, placing them around him and they are the quilt that warms him on those nights.

⟋

Deep into the nights, while the tourists lie quietly asleep, he reads Baldwin aloud to himself on the steps of the Lincoln Memorial.

This is where he befriends a homeless man, more than twice his age, and they talk literature at the marble feet of the man who wrote the Gettysburg Address. One night, when the homeless man tells of his brother, a doctor in Tennessee, the American asks why he doesn't ask for help.

"Pride," the man answers simply.

He says nothing.

"This surprises you?"

"I knew a homeless man in Ohio and he said the same thing."

"You seem like a proud person yourself."

He wishes to be left alone with his book and the solitude of the still warm night.

"Where's your home?"

"I have a room in Arlington."

"No, I mean your home."

"A small town in Pennsylvania. I never really fit in there; it was my father's hometown. Do you know that I was thirteen the first time I talked with a black person?"

"And now you're here talkin' to me and reading brother James Baldwin a few steps away from where Reverend Martin once had a dream."

He stares at the Reflecting Pool. Thinks of the fragility of the frayed string that separates the two of them.

"You may have a bed to sleep in, but you're just as homeless as me."

They look at each other.

"Where're you running to next?"

"I'm not sure."

Sixteen months later, he steps foot in Gaza for the first time.

A Four Cigarette Story

It is a fossil-dry August morning and Abu Khalil is in the back of his house, on the sixth rung of the eleven rung ladder, loosening the fake cement block, behind which he hides his books. He removes a much-used *Hamlet* and a recently obtained copy of Orwell's *1984*, leans over and hands the two books, with the care of passing an egg, to his youngest son, then replaces the thin piece of wood, painted gray with pockmarks, into the space, where its fits snugly. Before climbing down the ladder, Abu Khalil admires the work he has done; the memories of the numerous times that the army came in searching for the banned books, and never finding a one, etches a wrinkled smile of satisfaction across his face. His son sees the smile and knows what his father is thinking.

"Thank you, son. I will see you after lunch."

"Bye, Father."

Abu Khalil smells the bread and knows that it is ready. He steps into the heat and his wife holds out the large flatbread, two pieces in her left hand, atop which he places the books, and then she tops the books with another two pieces of the bread.

"Sandwiches for the intelligent," he says, as always, to his wife. "I will be home in time for my afternoon nap."

She watches her husband go down the street, unknowing that these are the final words of his own that she will ever hear him speak.

⌐

Abu Khalil turns right past the Martyrs' Cemetery. Should have encouraged my sons to carry shovels, rather than books, he thinks, stealing a corner of the bread and savoring it in his right cheek. As always, when a military jeep passes, Abu Khalil grabs his crotch and spits at the passing soldiers. Trying his best not to allow the sight of them to rankle him, he thinks that, after delivering the books to the young philosophy student at the University, two pieces of bread will be his and that if he hurries they will still be warm and perfect with his mint tea at his friend's house. The jeep is thrown into reverse and two soldiers spring out of the back and their guns are glaring at him.

"Drop the bread!"

Before doing so, Abu Khalil takes a vicious bite from the top piece, chewing as he watches, in slow motion, the bread and books separate as they fall to the street. One of the soldiers kicks aside the bread, nearly breaking Abu Khalil's heart. The soldier then picks up the two books and takes them to the jeep. The driver looks them over, climbs out of the jeep and approaches Abu Khalil. He holds out the books, Shakespeare in his left, Orwell his right, and points Abu Khalil to the middle of the road. He stands there watching the soldiers round up men and children, old and young, women heading to and from the market, halting cars and carts alike. The soldiers force the crowd to encircle Abu Khalil. A few faces he recognizes and he turns his head to his sandals; his tongue discovers a morsel of bread in the hole of his back right molar and he finds comfort in it.

Suddenly, *Hamlet* is held before him. He looks at the worn cover, the spine of which has threads hanging bare and tousled in the air. The soldier opens the book, rips out the title page and holds it an inch from Abu Khalil's face, so close that the letters have blurred.

"Eat it, old man."

He cannot believe what he is hearing, first the words old man—I am only forty-eight, he thinks—and then what they are asking him to do. He recalls the sheep he saw, many years ago, nosing through the garbage in the camp and finally settling on a sheet of a lampoon.

Still not looking up, he shakes his head in refusal.

Placing the book under his chin, the soldier lifts Abu Khalil's head.

"Fifty-eight pages, front and back," he says. "For each you do not eat we take one of these people with us."

He opens his mouth. The soldier hands him the title page.

"I will not feed you."

Abu Khalil takes the thin, fragile paper and stuffs it into his mouth. Brittle, it crumbles and the brown edges disintegrate and it reminds him of the burnt edges of the thin, cracker bread, *rokak*.

He hears the tearing of another page and then another and he doesn't need to count the number of pages he has eaten. The sentences he can taste, the words, the letters, the commas, and he can feel them saunter down his throat and into his stomach. Scene by scene. Act by act.

⟋

They leave him standing there, the cover of the book at his feet, the crowd of onlookers scattering, in disbelief of what they have just seen. The jeep roars away and leaves everything quiet, at least in Abu Khalil's head. He remains there, awaiting the inevitable knifing pain in his stomach, or for his bowels to loosen right there on the street. Nothing happens. In fact, he feels fine, as good as he felt when he left the house that morning. Someone puts an arm around him and asks if he would like to sit down, or go to the clinic, or home. He shakes his head no to all of them and begins retracing his steps of earlier that morning. No one gets too close to him, as though he is a kind of djinn or crazed conjurer. But they are there, a lot of people, those who have witnessed what has just happened or already have heard about it as word gallops through Jabaliya.

He turns onto School Street, pulled by the redundancy of a lifetime he has walked this route. In his dreamlike state, he nearly collides with his son and wife. Each takes an arm and they ask question after question, none of which he responds to.

⟋

Not a sound comes from his mouth as the afternoon segues into night. There is no pain and, as with that morning, calm is a tranquilizer, leaving him, if anything, a bit catatonic. There have been many visitors, for the most part, well-wishers with genuine concern, but, of course, also those being outright nosy. Abu Khalil's family thanks everyone, keeping them at the entrance before politely shutting the door. But the knocks become more and more and finally Abu Khalil's son places a sign on the door, telling everyone they will talk with them in the morning.

That night, however, before the dawn dissolves the dark, an unusual thing happens.

Abu Khalil, his throat papyrus-parched, leaves his sleeping mat and drinks from the bowl of his hands, over and over, a stream of handfuls. Quietly, he goes to the back of the house, places the ladder against the wall and by feel removes the fake cement block. He takes the first book he touches, fingers the cover and turns to the opening page, which he rips out, paying no heed to the noise, and nibbles at its edges, before devouring it.

From the doorway of her room, his wife asks the question that every wife would ask if they saw their husband up a ladder, nibbling on a book, at that hour of night, "What are you doing?"

Abu Khalil pauses, taking his time to swallow the last of the page. He clears his throat and recites, as much to the wall as to his wife, the first verse of Shakespeare she has ever heard:

> Whether 'tis nobler in the mind to suffer
> The slings and arrows of outrageous fortune,
> Or to take arms against a sea of troubles,
> And by opposing, end them?

Before her husband finishes with the verse, his wife goes and wakes their son.

Thus begins the strange days that follow. Abu Khalil, whenever he speaks, recites only the pages he has eaten. At meals, his wife begins to serve, along with bowls of cucumbers and sardines and tomatoes, a bowl with a page or two from one of the books, torn into bite-size pieces. Once, Abu Khalil's son pinches, with a piece of bread, a shred of the paper. He eats them together and is afraid to speak, but when he does, normal words come out of his mouth, words no different than he has spoken his entire life. Still, he doesn't eat any more of the pages.

Nor are the nights diffident to strangeness.

In the middle hours of the night, Abu Khalil joins the black-hooded graffiti artists, and on the cement block canvas of the camp, after they have painted their red, black, green and white maps, he recites a line or two from one of the books and they paint them across the pictures.

Each morning, Abu Khalil revisits the walls of the night before and admires what they have created; he makes sure that he is there early, for within hours of daylight the whitewash of the soldiers muffles the walls until they are free to speak again that night.

⚊

Secrets are as fleeting as the days of spring in Jabaliya.

Within weeks a convoy of jeeps stalks the street and surrounds Abu Khalil's house. Tear gas is dropped between the roof and wall and flushes out his family. With spotlights shining, as though the full moon has fallen and become hung up in a tree, Abu Khalil and his family are lined against the wall and forced to watch as the bulldozer compresses their house. His heart moans, but is soon comforted by the thought that almost all the banned words are inside him.

But the back wall doesn't fall. The bulldozer can't bring it down, nor does the bomb placed at its base. Hours pass and the neighborhood is left in rubble. Abu Khalil is taken away and, in the upcoming days, his family clears out enough of the destroyed house to where they can pitch a tent and that is where they remain until new walls can be constructed and a thin roof, once again, placed above their heads.

⚊

At the military compound, Abu Khalil is on a chair in the middle of a brightly lit room. His hands are tied behind the chair and the bare bulb dangles inches from his head. He has been in this position for hours and has not spoken a word. Even the military's top interrogator cannot extract a syllable from his mouth.

Finally, they untie his raw wrists and leave him alone with a book leaning against the far wall. Abu Khalil, after only a few minutes, cannot stand the taunting book and he lunges at it. Paying no attention, he rips out a handful of pages and gorges himself on them. Two, sometimes three pages at a time, he eats, ignoring the texture of the pages—a newer book, with a sheen coating them, more difficult to chew and swallow than those back in his house. Soon he finishes. Braced against the wall, he feels sick to his stomach and pregnant with guilt.

He thinks he is going to cry, but instead of tears, words rise up, like bile, and he shouts them and the louder he shouts the more they scour his throat and they pound off the walls and only grow louder for they have nowhere to escape.

⌐

When hearing the words from the interrogation room, the soldiers are elated; the rumors of this man who eats words and recites them verbatim turn out to be true. They wait until Abu Khalil exhausts himself, but the wait is long. Days pass, dozens of times he recites *The Occupation Handbook* before slumping to the floor. The soldiers allow him to rest and they feed him two times a day.

One morning, several weeks later, they lead him out of the room and gently into the back of a jeep, holding his head down so he doesn't bump it. They drive the coastal road and enter Jabaliya from the west. Before turning past the market, the soldier in the back hands Abu Khalil a second copy of *The Occupation Handbook* and he eats it slowly. Waiting for him to finish, they drive several times around the camp. Stones from the youth pelt the jeep.

He finishes. The jeep heads up School Street and stops under the willow. A couple of men sitting against the tree are grabbed and, along with Abu Khalil, are used as human shields. But not a stone or shoe or Molotov cocktail is thrown, nor are any words launched at the soldiers; some of those gripping stones drop them in their shock, the words sons of whores fall harmlessly to the street below. Everyone listens to Abu Khalil reciting, with such passion, in the language of the soldiers, the words of humiliation, words that if any son or daughter of yours spoke them, you would not hesitate to take a knife or pair of scissors and promptly sever their tongues so they could speak no more.

⌐

The black hooded men do not even wait until night to come and haul Abu Khalil away. His family offers no resistance as a filthy towel is shoved into his mouth, leaving only the muffled shadows of his words. He is thrown into the back of the car and it vanishes up the street.

⌐

Even after all this time, more than fifteen years since Abu Khalil was taken, and six years since the military has left, the back wall of the house still stands. The ladder is braced against the wall and every once in a while someone will climb it, to the fifth or sixth or seventh rung, depending on how tall they are, and they will place their ear against the fake cement block and listen to Abu Khalil's voice reciting all the books he ate. Others from the camp go to the beach at night, the part of the beach that is closest to the border, and from there they listen to him speak in the language of the waves. More and more people from Jabaliya can be seen gathering under the giant willow, where you can hear his tears fall before being swallowed by the ground.

Back in Jabaliya, he opens his eyes to the night, surrounded by three generations of sleeping men, and he hears the footsteps of Bassam and goes out of the bedroom and joins him. The both of them pace the cement floor and then make some sweet mint tea and they drink it in the darkness, neither of them divulging what it is that keeps them from sleeping on this night.

Every ten days or so the American begins to feel the crush of the camp, the smother of its walls, the heckling of the curfew, the utter lack of ever being alone. He imagines climbing the giant willow, way up into the highest point of its umbrella, and sitting there with the ebb and flow of Jabaliya far off below.

Twice a month he goes the fifty miles to Jerusalem to get a reprieve from the claustrophobia of this place. After passing through the hour long wait at the border, with every road sign along the way, the driver begins his lament:

Dimra.
Najd.
Dayr Sunayd.
Simsim.
Burayr.
Bayt Jirja.
Barbara.
Bayt Timra.
Al-Jiyya
Hirbiya.
Kawkaba.

Some of the names he recognizes: Simsim and Kawkaba and, of course, Burayr, only eight miles from block number four, the town of the family he lives with. He thinks of the many times, on the many journeys in his life, that he has walked this far—eight miles—and how frighteningly close it can be, and how great a distance.

A cold rain pelts Jerusalem, chasing the last of winter away.

He ducks into a basement bar, dripping water on the spiral cement steps. A dungeon-like place. Bob Marley's lyrics of freedom and the psychopathic strobe lights pull the American down the steps. The lights make it difficult to see and at first he thinks that the dancing soldiers playing their Kalashnikovs as guitars is a mirage.

It is not and he walks away from the strumming soldiers and to the counter where he orders a beer. Many of the patrons wear army fatigues and are in a festive mood, dancing and singing along to Marley. He takes a drink and imagines the sound of the rain pinging the tin roofs of Jabaliya and the blurry reception of the Egyptian soap opera and his mat in the sleeping room, where, on this night, Mustafa, the youngest in the family, will most likely sleep once again, the room where he has slept all his life until the American arrived.

He regrets coming here and feels the tightening of its walls and the lights and the music drumming at his head and even more, the guilt. A soldier leans on the counter and looks at the stranger.

"To Mandela," he says, lifting his drink.

The American gives him a baffled look. The soldier leans closer and shouts.

"Mandela has been freed after twenty-seven years in prison!" Again the soldier raises his glass.

He isn't sure what to say, what to do. He calculates the years—1963 he was imprisoned, more than a dozen years after the opening of Jabaliya.

The American looks at the soldier, who still holds his glass aloft. He wants to say—I know the truth. I have been to Ramallah and Hebron and Nablus and Bethlehem and to each of the eight camps in Gaza. I know the truth, he wants to say. I know of places where children, because of years of nighttime curfews, have never seen the moon or a shooting star. He hates himself, hates his weakness in front of the soldier. A devouring hopelessness crumbles him and he understands now that what he feels is only a slice of the hopelessness endured all over Gaza and the West Bank. It is paralyzing, unforgiving, an exhausting way to live one's life. Like driving on ice.

He manages to turn away from the soldier and look at the crowd of people, people between him and the stairs, stairs that will lead him out into the lashing rain, rain that he cannot wait until it slaps him coldly in the face.

～

The rain of the night before has let up, but the day is still dreary. On his way to the taxi to await a ride back to Gaza, the American stops at a food stall in the Old City of Jerusalem.

The balding older man is carving some chicken from the spit into a platter.

"Can I have a large chicken shwarma?"

Without turning around, the man asks:

"What part of the states are you from?"

"Pennsylvania."

He cuts the top of the pita bread and squeezes it to make a pocket.

"What do you think of our beautiful country?"

He remembers the bar and the soldiers celebrating the night before.

"I have been living in Gaza."

The man doesn't react. He continues to fill the sandwich with chicken and lettuce and tomato and pickles.

"Tahina?"

"Excuse me."

"Would you like tahina sauce?"

"Yes, please. Only a little."

The man adds the sauce, wraps the sandwich, and, as he hands it to the American, the left sleeve of his jacket slides above his wrist. As the American gives him the money, he notices the tattooed letter "A," followed by the number "1." The crinkle of the paper bag rips his eyes from the man's left arm. He takes the bag and begins his journey back to Gaza.

～

The American returns to Jerusalem twice more before he leaves Gaza forever. He spends his days roaming the stone streets in the four quarters of the Old City—Muslim, Jewish, Christian, Armenian. For breakfast, he eats sesame bread with a packet of spices while sitting atop the steps outside of Damascus Gate. The routines are comforting, but now he finds himself looking more closely at those passing by, at those folding up prayer notes and placing them into the cracks of the Western Wall, staring at shopkeepers. But instead of studying the faces of the people, he searches their left arms for numbers hiding beneath the crawl of a sleeve.

--

My Father, the Mole

For many months I have wondered why my father no longer brings home with him the smell of sardines, and with it the silver flakes that fleck his brown skin, and the grit of sand that sometimes sprinkles into the small dish of olive oil in which we dab our breakfast bread; instead, it is a reddish clay that mats itself to my father's jeans, and pries its way under his nails, both fingers and toes—all this leaves me feeling that the man across from me is not really my father at all.

But today is my birthday—my tenth—and I don't think about any of this. It is half an hour into dawn and I sit facing my father, a small tray, holding silver bowls of scrambled eggs, tomatoes, and cucumbers, is on the floor between us. I am up early because Father will take me in the direction of the Sinai, where my present awaits.

Every year is the same, my gift in the direction of south. Recounting from last year until my sixth birthday, which is as far back as I can remember, I think of the gift that has awaited me. A video arcade. A day at the beach. A night sleeping on Father's fishing boat. Tasting ice cream for the first time—mint. I know better than to ask what the present is; I hurry up and eat as fast as I can.

"Slow down, Zaid. There are still eighteen hours left of your birthday. Whatever is at the border will be there when we arrive."

Those words—at the border—stop me. I place my piece of flatbread on the tray and try imagining what those three simple words could possibly mean. I have never been there, only to the town, Rafah, and the refugee camp of the same name. Again, I run back through the previous birthdays, and yes, it is a fact, that each year my father takes me further from Jabaliya. This year, the border itself. Slow down your thoughts, I tell myself, keep to your tenth, not eleventh, birthday. But the thought won't leave me alone: could it be that next year Father will take me across the border, into Egypt itself? Is that even possible?

My mother snaps me from my reverie with a kiss on the forehead. I welcome the warm kiss, glad that she does so in the privacy of the house and not in front of my friends, which, although I am older now, she still sometimes does.

"A hundred more birthdays, my son, if Allah wills it."

One hundred and ten, I think, I would be one hundred and ten if Allah so wishes. Only the man down the street, Abu Hassan, is anywhere near that age—eighty-five, perhaps as much as ninety—and look at him: what little hair he has is white; the wrinkles on his forehead are like the waves of the sea; I have had twice as many birthdays as he teeth in that head of his.

"Are you finished eating, Zaid?" my father asks.

"Yes. I think we should go."

"Put this on." My mother helps me into my jean jacket. "It will be cool today."

It is early still and a light fog has softened the giant willow making it appear as though it is a shadow. As we walk past the school, where I am in the fourth grade, I wish, although I know it is wrong to do so, that it wasn't so early in the morning and we would pass some of my friends, at least one of them, and a pang of envy would trundle through them for just this one day. By the time we arrive at the market, I have squelched this idea and my father finds a taxi and we go the nineteen miles in the direction of the Sinai.

⌐

The somnolent sheath of fog has lifted by the time we arrive near the border, forty-five minutes later. When I see boys my age, carrying backpacks, I think of my best friend, Mustafa, and how, each morning, we meet and walk together to school. We have been friends since I can remember; Mustafa, with his funny bent left ear, which my grandmother says came from him sleeping so much, as a baby, on his left side.

Together, the two of us wear our flour-white shirts and neckties for the festival of Eid. We share bites of one another's ice cream, pass on the book we have just finished reading. As my father and I get out of the taxi, I think of how, right now, Mustafa is walking down School Street, maybe even sitting in the classroom, with math about to begin. And just as I am thinking of him, he is probably thinking of me.

As my father takes my hand, and we walk through the streets, I wonder what the hands of other fathers feel like, say, the hands of a lawyer or teacher or martyr. My father's hands are those of a laborer and the calluses, for him, are like the rings of a tree. Thirty-four rings, my father.

We go into the market where normally I want to stop and marvel at the colors and shapes and smells, but the thoughts of where and what my gift might be are a distraction. As if on cue, like magic, my father answers my thoughts, something I both love and hate when he does it.

"A little further, just on the other side of the market."

"Can we see Egypt from where we are going?"

"Something even better."

What could possibly be better than seeing another country? Going there, of course, but I know that is not possible with the blockade on Gaza, now in its seventh year. To see another country would begin to answer some of my questions, questions Mustafa and I talk about, and the same ones I sometimes think of alone at night. Is their soil the same color as ours? How about the sky? The sea? The crispness of their *falafel*?

"Over there. We are going over there."

I see nothing that looks like a birthday present, just a few white tents and clusters of men smoking and chatting. My father looks down at me, a slice of a grin on his face, but not a word is spoken. One of the men motions to my father, and then another and yet another, until the huddled group of five or six all acknowledge him. We join the men, and although they throw a glance my way, none of them says anything to me. Don't they know it's my birthday, and why doesn't my father say something to them? As the men talk, my father lets go of my hand and this makes me feel even more isolated.

"Have you heard anything?"

"No, but it should be soon," the man with a walkie-talkie says.

"Yes, but anything could happen, as we know all too well."

I try focusing on the conversation, searching for any hint that could tell something of what is awaiting me, but their words are much like the smoke they blow into the morning air, there one second, gone the next.

I look off into the distance, about fifty yards away, where there is a fence with barbed wire strung atop it. That must be the border, I think, and I try to get a better glimpse of it through the fence. The men are still talking and I walk away from my father.

"Don't go too far, Zaid."

"I won't," I answer and I don't, going not more than twenty steps away to where the tent doesn't obstruct my view. But it isn't all that much better from here, for there is a girl standing atop an overturned blue milk crate. I imagine that she is seeing a hundred things that I have never seen, but it is my birthday and it should be me seeing them, not her. I am about to turn and go back to my father when she speaks.

"Hi."

The single word startles me. I cannot move; it is as though I am stuck in knee-deep muck and when I hear her laugh it is even more impossible to do so.

"Why aren't you in school?" Her voice is like that of a lemon, or a lime, if either of them could speak—sour, pinched in the throat, but refreshing.

"It's my birthday," I say, turning around. Now that she is close by and standing on the ground, I can see that she is shorter than me. I want to ask why she isn't in school, but dare not do so.

"My birthday isn't until March. I'll be thirteen."

Thirteen, I think, so much older than me. Then suddenly, somehow, my birthday has lost its significance and I don't want to be talking with her anymore. I am walking away when she stops me again. This time she says nothing, but it is her movement that keeps me locked to the ground and I can't pry my eyes from her, although, over and over voices in my head are yelling that it is not polite to look, even a peek is rude, but staring as you are now is unmentionable. I imagine my father seeing me gawking at this girl—today two years older than me—but in a few short months, three years older, making it all the more rude, but I can't force my head to turn away from her as she lifts the bottom of her dirty brown robe and adjusts, left then right, the bottom half of her legs. She does so as if it is the most natural thing to do, standing there as if she were simply tying a shoe. For the first time, I notice a pair of metal crutches on the ground.

"I stepped on a cluster bomb," she says, with the same casualness as she adjusted those legs.

I am still staring.

"I'm sorry," is all I can think of saying.

"It's okay. It happened when I was five, so I am used to it. Anyway, I have to go to work. You can stand on the crate for a couple of minutes if you want; you can get a better view of the sea from there," she says, picking up the crutches.

"Thanks," I say, but now I cannot look at her at all as if she has disappeared along with her legs.

I go over to the milk crate and step atop it. As she said, there is a nice view.

"Happy birthday," she says and I thank her without looking around.

A minute passes before I glance over my shoulder and notice that she is no longer there; I can't find her until she waves to me from the entrance to the market, thirty yards away, where she is sitting on the ground next to a banana and date stall, which I think she is working at, until a woman bends down and gives her a coin and a handful of dates. I can see her thanking the woman and next to her, leaning against the stall, are her crutches.

My father's voice rescues me and I jump from the crate and run to him. There is a commotion coming from the direction of one of the white tents and my father takes me to where about a dozen men are around it. There is an opening, a large hole in the ground beneath the tent. One man is reaching down into the opening, so far down, that his head and chest and stomach disappear while another man has ahold of him as though trying to keep him from being swallowed by the hole.

"It's all right, Zaid. The man has him and he will not fall."

I want to tell my father that I know this, although I really don't.

"I have it," yells a voice inside the tunnel. "Pull me up!"

My father goes over to the tunnel and grabs the man by the waist while the other still has ahold of his legs. The face of my father is red from exertion and his eyes are bigger than normal, looking like he did on those mornings he used to take me with him to the market and he strained while hauling those large baskets of fish. Although my father's face looks like that, this place is nothing at all like the market—smells nothing like it, has none of its constant commotion, certainly not the colors. Somehow this place seems secretive.

I see the head of the large cat first and it looks as though the man's body has now taken on this face, but soon I see the man's face next to it, not red, like my father's, purple almost. The man is full out of the tunnel's mouth now, yet still my father has him by the waist, as if he is preventing him from running away with the enormous cat. But I can see now that the cat will not run away, not because the man has it, but because it appears dead; eyes closed, giant paws dangling from long legs, mouth open a bit, a little of its pink, fleshy tongue slipping out. Father has let go of the man and he walks toward me, the man with the cat next to him. I take a couple of steps back, before bumping into the man with the walkie-talkie.

"Happy birthday," he says.

My father repeats the words and the other men also join in the chorus and I don't know what to feel or say. My first thought is that the cat is too big for our house and where would it sleep; probably in the front room where mother keeps her loom to make and sell her carpets. But I can't imagine Mother allowing that, for she rarely permits me to go in there, and never alone, only when she or Father is with me. The man with the cat bends down and I can hear its soft purr and now I am certain that the cat is not dead, just asleep.

"Go ahead, Zaid, pet him," my father says.

As if to show me it is all right to do so he touches the cat atop its head. I hesitate and my father takes my hand and places it on the animal's head, which is larger than both my father's and my hand together. The cat is the color of the school ground, not during the rainy months of winter, when it is a dark brown and sticky, but of summer, after the sun has been beating down upon it. The fur is not as soft as that of the cat I sometimes see running across the metal rooftops of Jabaliya.

"You are the first boy in Gaza to touch a lion, Zaid," the man says.

The word *lion* jerks away my hand. The men, including my father, laugh.

"It's okay, he's asleep."

"I thought it was a cat."

"Well, it is a cat, just a big one."

"How are we going to take him home?"

"We're not taking him home. I just brought you here for your birthday."

"Then where are they taking him?"

"To the zoo, Zaid. And that's where we are going. You are going to take the first lion in Gaza to the zoo."

⸺

We are walking away from the tunnel and the man continues to hold the sleeping lion in his arms. Again, I have my father's hand and I am tortured by the thought of the lion waking up and how it would tear apart the men, like the lions I heard about in stories. Unexpectedly, I ask my father:

"I want to show the lion to that girl over there."

My father looks to where I am pointing. There are other people there, but only one girl and I'm certain my father knows who I am speaking of.

"I don't think that's possible, son. We need to get the lion to the zoo before she wakes up."

"But she has no legs."

"What do you mean no legs?"

"The girl. She stepped on a bomb."

"Zaid, we…"

"Please, Father."

My father calls to the man ahead of us and they talk for a short time. They look at the lion and then at me.

"Okay, but quickly," the man says to me, more serious than angry.

We arrive beside the girl before she notices us.

"Would you like to see the first lion in Gaza?"

She answers as if she had been waiting for the question.

"Sure."

The man with the lion bends down and brings it close to the girl. She reaches out, not hesitating at all. Softly she touches the head and back of the lion. I watch the hand move overtop the lion and the girl seems happy and I look up to my father and then to the man holding the lion and they, too, appear happy; even the lion seems peaceful. The thought that the lion will wake up no longer agonizes me, for I am certain that as long as the girl continues to pet the lion that peace will reign.

⌒

We ride in the front of the pickup truck with the groggy lion in a cage in the back. Through the window, I see into the truck's cabin. My father tells me that kneeling on the seat, and looking through the window that way, would be easier. I do that and slowly the lion becomes more alert as the drugs begin to wear off. She opens her eyes—the man told me that the lion is female and that they hope to have a male in the zoo next month—and what were a few minutes earlier slivers of greenish-brown have become larger orbs, and they continue to grow until they are as big as the spoons we will use later tonight to eat the *couscous* my mother is now at home preparing for dinner.

My face is less than three feet from the lion's and my breath has steamed the window, but when I pull back a little the steam evaporates in seconds. We stare at each other and I think that she is really nothing at all like the lions I have read about in books—ferocious and terrifying, with mouths so big and teeth so sharp that they gobble children in one clean sweep. When I first believed she was a cat, I thought she was huge, but after finding out she is a lion, she began to look different, small almost. Her eyes have a milky look to them and there are tiny dots in the middle as though someone has taken a pen and drawn them there. My father and the man, Shafiq, whom he has introduced as the veterinarian at the zoo, are talking, but I pay them little attention.

Without warning, and impossible as it may seem, the lion's eyes grow even larger, as though they are eating away at her face. Suddenly, and with great force, the lion springs from its crouch and smacks the cage, throwing it against the window. I feel it against my face and I fly backward, out of fright more than the force, losing my balance and hitting against the dashboard, then half-falling between the seat and floor.

"What is it, Zaid?" my father asks, and begins to laugh when he realizes what has happened. The driver also laughs and I climb back onto the seat between the two men. I sit there with my eyes locked straight ahead, not daring to look through the cabin window. The whole time, however, something is twisting my head trying to force me to look again at the lion. I am convinced that she has broken through the cage and is now racing in the opposite direction along Salahadin Road to the border and when she gets there she will thrust aside the workers and jump into the tunnel and return to where she came from.

And it is with this thought—I am not sure why it has taken so long to realize—that I understand why my father no longer comes home smelling like the sea and why he has this red soil under his nails and on his clothes. He is one of the tunnel workers. My father is looking at me when I turn to him and he smiles and gives my hair a rustle. I hear the cage in the back of the truck rattling and I spin around, not kneeling on the seat as before, just turning enough to see the lion hitting into the cage with her paws and I think that she will tire herself out just like my mother tells me that my little sister, when she is throwing a tantrum, will tire herself out and fall asleep.

"We're here," my father says.

I watch as the truck passes by the entrance of the Gaza Zoo. I have never been here before; some kids at school have talked about the zoo, which has been open for more than a year. A few months ago the United Nations gave out day passes, but I didn't get one. We drive slowly past cages—ponies and birds and monkeys and goats—and at each one I can see that the animals are restless and uneasy. Some make noises, especially the birds and monkeys, others just look anxious as they pace back and forth. I think that the lion is growling at them, but when I look at her I see that she is silent, but staring at the other animals with those eyes that both frighten and enrapture me.

The truck is backed up to a large cage with its gate open.

"Stay in here, Zaid, until we get the lion into her cage, then we'll take a look around the zoo."

My father climbs onto the bed of the truck and I am again on my knees watching through the cabin window. The lion is on all fours and I can see how small the cage is. My father pushes the cage while the driver pulls on it, getting it closer to the back of the truck. With one quick motion the driver flips the lock and the lion springs out and into the larger zoo cage. And now I again hear the stirring of other animals and feel their terror that they have for this newest member in the zoo.

I think of Mustafa and how it is nearly lunch and tonight, when I get home, he will come to our house and celebrate my birthday and I can tell him and all the others at school tomorrow of how I touched this most fearsome of animals and how I helped to bring him from his homeland, so very far away, into our world of Gaza.

⸺

As I look at her through the cage, the lion again appears small. She is at the back, half-hidden behind a rock, devouring, with large teeth, a dead chicken. From where I am, I can hear the crunching of the chicken bones. It is both horrifying and thrilling. As she eats, her eyes are smaller than when I saw them though the cabin window, and when the sun hits them at a certain angle, their color wavers from a light brown to a milky green and somewhere in between the two.

"Where is she from?" I ask my father standing next to me.

"Africa, I imagine."

"How long have you been working in the tunnels?"

"How do you know that is where I work?"

"I figured it out today."

"Almost six months now, since I lost my job fishing. I am lucky; a lot of men don't have a job."

The lion comes out from behind the rock and stalks around. I cannot tell if she is angry or lonely; it seems as if every time I see her she changes. She looks at my father and I wonder if she recognizes us.

"Do you like working in the tunnels?"

"It is very different from fishing where you are surrounded by the vastness of the water. Inside the tunnels, it is very narrow and you have to crawl most of the time."

"How can you bring such big animals through them?"

"They put the animals to sleep, like they did the lion, and bring them through one of the larger tunnels. Some of the tunnels are big enough to bring cars through. Don't get too close to the cage."

My father and I take a couple of steps away as the lion nears. She doesn't growl but rather makes a low gurgling sound from her throat. Her paws are very large, but as she passes they seem soft on the bottom, like bread dough, and I wish that I had touched them to see if it were true. Each step she takes, however, her claws, long and sharp, poke out, threateningly. The whole day is as if a dream and it is hard to fathom that only a few hours ago I petted her. As she gets closer to the front of the cage, the monkeys and peacocks across the way become more agitated. I take my father's hand and we go over to the monkeys. One of the bigger monkeys sits above a smaller one and plucks at its head and back, eating the insects that it picks. The monkeys pay us little attention; their focus is on the lion, behind us now.

"I think we should be heading back. Your mother is preparing dinner for you."

I look to the sky and see that evening is rapidly approaching. If this were summer, we would have several more hours of daylight and could perhaps even go to the beach. We turn from the monkeys and head toward the gate. One final time I look back at the lion, but cannot see her. I know that by the time we arrive in Jabaliya it will be dark and that there will be no moon on this night, for the new moon will not be out until Saturday. I think of the girl and wonder if she is still begging for money and whether or not, when she goes to sleep, she wears the legs that are, at the same time, both hers and not hers.

~

I will not see the lion again until the following summer.

On the school grounds a few of us are playing soccer, not a match, but just shooting at the goal from various angles and distances. I have won the game and Hatem, an older boy who doesn't like to lose, comes over and says that although I was the first to pet the lion, that he also touched it, which was now much larger than when I did so, more than eight months before.

"I even have a photo of me with the lion!"

"You talk too much."

"It's at my house. I'll show you the photo for an ice cream."

"Okay," I say, no longer really doubting his claim, but wanting to see the picture. "Let me see the photo first."

We hurry to block number nine where Hatem lives.

"Wait out here. My father doesn't want me to be showing the photo to anyone."

I am the only one of my friends who has come along; the others have stayed at the school grounds. I wait and the heat tires me, so I go across the street to the wall and sit against its two o'clock-wide shadow. Even in the shade the heat lashes me. Through my ever-growing tired eyes, people pass as though through a mist. A horse-drawn cart clicks by, unreal, as though it is walking through butter. I shut my eyes, the hot shade an unwanted quilt atop me. Everything is heavy—my hair, my ears, even the drops of sweat that slither down my neck, down my back. I have lost track of time and may have even slept a little while when I am shaken by Hatem.

"You owe me an ice cream." He is holding a photo, one of poor quality, with him, his arm around a lion. It is one of the pictures with a date on it: 6-20-07. Hatem seems uncomfortable in the photo, stilted. I take the picture and study it closely. The lion is certainly the one I petted on my birthday. Her eyes, although they look distant and sad, are those that I stared into so often that day. She has grown to nearly twice the size of when she was brought through the tunnels.

"Give me back the picture and let's get that ice cream."

"Just a minute."

I look closer at the lion and see that she is not the same; something is different about her. Behind Hatem and the lion is a backdrop that looks like a savannah. There is a beautiful tree silhouetted by an orange sunset. But that is not what makes her different.

"Where did you get this picture taken?"

"In Gaza City."

"At the zoo?"

"No, at a building, like a big photo studio."

"When?"

"A couple of weeks ago. What's with all the questions? Come on, let's go."

I return the photo, still not certain of what it is about the lion that doesn't seem right. He hides it in the back pocket of his jeans and goes to his house. I check to make sure I have money for the ice cream and remain in the shade waiting for Hatem to come out.

⚊

Father is late arriving home and I feel the tension in the way mother prepares dinner. The chopping of the spinach has a roughness to it; her kneading knuckles press deeper into the dough; the lid of a pan rattles more than usual. There are many possibilities for Father to be not on time: he had to work late; he had to wait for a taxi; the battery in his phone has died again. But I can sense Mother thinking the worst. I avoid her, wishing I hadn't stopped playing so early. In my room, I wonder about what Father may have brought through the tunnels today. Some evenings, when my mother is working on the loom, Father will tell of what happened in the tunnels. As of late he rarely brings animals into Gaza, although there have been a few—a gazelle, a peacock, and a couple of monkeys within the past months. The animals are much too expensive to bring through the tunnels so Father hauls other goods: cigarettes, kerosene, medicine, and one day he came home all excited for he had driven a car beneath the border.

Father tells me of his days when Mother is not around; she doesn't like to hear anything about his work, dreading that he will someday not come home, for a growing number of tunnel-workers are being killed in collapses or in military missile strikes. When my father says goodbye to us in the morning, my mother's mood changes and remains edgy until he walks in at night.

This is how it is tonight until the door opens and I run out of my room to greet Father. But I stop, for there is something in his silence with Mother and they just look at each other and he glances at me, but turns away, and the two of them go into the front room where the carpet-loom is, and they close the door severing me from them. Quietly I go there and stand to the side of the door from where I can hear, not voices, for my parents are not speaking, but crying. And even the crying is muffled, as though there is a pillow or something smothering it. I step out of my sandals, so that they will not flop as I walk away, but there are voices now, also muffled, but clear enough.

"All for a sheep..." my father's voice cracks.

"Ali. Ali. Ali," my mother's voice quivers as she repeats my father's name as though it is the verse to a song or a prayer.

"All for a sheep. What the hell do we need another damn sheep for in this place?"

My father's words stun me. Never have I heard him speak like this. I force myself to step away and go to my room, wanting to close the door, but afraid that its hinges will squeal. I leave it open and wait, knowing that when my parents emerge from the other room that things will never quite be the same.

⌇

It is a month since my father's friend died in a tunnel collapse and summer has nearly fled Jabaliya and soon school will begin. Father no longer works in the tunnels, but most mornings he goes somewhere until evening.

I am up early the next day and have breakfast with him.

"What are you going to do today?"

"Probably play soccer this morning before it gets too hot."

"You have to go back to school Monday; maybe we can visit the zoo this week. Would you like that?"

"Yeah, sure." I hope that my voice doesn't give away my apprehension, but Father seems distant these days, and I don't think he has noticed. I, too, am distracted as of late, especially this morning. My father kisses me atop the head and goes off to work, leaving me to the day ahead.

⌇

I have promised Hatem two ice creams if he shows me the place where he had his photo taken with the lion. We hop the back of a donkey cart and go more than halfway to the city. Hatem doesn't want to come in and he leaves for the market after pointing out the building to me.

I stand across the street, continuing to finger the coins in my pocket, while the voices inside my head argue over whether I should go into the building and have my picture taken with her. But I know that the only way that I can see her up close is to do so. It is this that shoves me across the street and into the building, inside which there is a large room with nothing in it other than a sofa sitting on a raised wooden floor. The room is surprisingly cool and I stand looking around.

"Welcome," a voice behind me says. I am not sure where the large-bellied man with the gray-black beard has come from, for I don't see a door other than the one I entered and I didn't hear him come in.

"Hello," is all I say.

"Are you here for a photo?"

"Yes."

"We have three animals today. A monkey, a parrot or the lion."

"The lion, please." I feel sweat forming on my forehead, but don't dare wipe it away.

He goes behind the sofa, and like magic, pulls down a screen with the same picture that was the backdrop for Hatem's photo. He shows me two other backdrops—a tangerine-red sunset and a picture of the sea.

"I like the first one."

"Yes, that is nice, especially with the lion. Okay, why don't you get settled on the sofa and I will bring her out."

He disappears through a door behind the screen with the sunset picture. I stare at the picture and wonder if this is really how the sun looks in other places and will I ever have the chance to see it. I am still standing when the man comes out, the lion with a chain around her neck. I can't believe how big she is. The man smiles through his beard and tells me not to worry, the lion has had her teeth removed. Now I know why the lion looked so different in the photo, and I can see it even more so in person. I have a hard time looking away from her large head, with its mouth sunken and hollow, and how sad she looks and this is what consumes me until I finally see the way she is walking, gingerly as though the slightest pressure causes excruciating pain. I see her paws, huge yet delicate, with their raw red holes where the claws used to be.

"Go on, get on the sofa."

I am feeling light-headed and confused and I take a step toward the sofa and when I look at the picture of the beautiful sunset I drop to the floor.

⚊

Staring down at me is not the toothless lion, nor the bearded man, but my father. Looking past him I do not see the familiarity of the corrugated roof of my house, but an unfamiliar ceiling and I am not on my mattress, but rather a sofa.

"Son. How are you feeling?"

I turn to my father and sit up, saying nothing. I don't see the lion; the bearded man is also gone and I wonder whether any of it actually happened. Then I see the picture of the sunset and know that it is true. But what is my father doing here? He looks away and I know that he understands what I am thinking.

"Here, take a drink." He hands me a half-filled bottle of warm water, still looking at the sunset, as am I. The water is good and I finish it.

"Do you want some more?"

I wonder what he is asking about, then, when he takes the bottle from me and walks away I understand that he meant water. I stand and feel fine. My father returns with the bottle, full now.

"Thank you." I drink more of the water, not only because it is refreshing, but also because it is a distraction.

"Abu Jabeer will give you a ride back to Jabaliya. I will be home later."

I hand my father the bottle.

"Take it with you," he says.

~

Father doesn't come home for dinner and without him we eat. Now that he no longer works in the tunnels, Mother seems calmer. When she is making her carpets, I head outside for a little while and watch the evening stroll up and down School Street. Soon I tire of this and sit in my room. I close the door and I'm still awake when I hear Father come in. The only light is that which peeks in through where the door is slightly open. I don't move as my father stands above my mattress. There is an itch on my cheek; I dare not quiet it. I feign sleep. My father feigns conversation. I listen to the indecipherable voices of our neighbors, the Kanafanis. My father opens the door halfway, and it stays like that for a moment, but like the itch that rages on my cheek, when he closes the door, both are no longer there.

~

Although my eleventh birthday is less than a week away, Father has made no mention of it, nor has my mother. As the days fold into weeks it has become easier to be with my father and not be harassed by thoughts of the lion. This doesn't mean that I never think of her, or that images of her do not invade my dreams. They do, but at times, more and more as of late, they are of that day when I first saw her come out of the tunnel. In these dreams so too is the girl—inseparable the both of them. How can they not be?

⌒

Some mornings, after my father returned to the camp from a night of fishing, he would come into my room and tell me of what he had caught. Many times it was the same story, for my father was a sardine fisherman, and his catch, for the most part, varied little. Before leaving my room, however, he would always tell me of the word he had caught that night in his net. *Hope. Forgiveness. Appreciation. Loyalty. Rebellion.* Make sure you eat all your breakfast, he would say as he left the room, your mother has taken great care cooking *forgiveness* into the food.

On other mornings, my father would have the word written on a piece of paper and he would give it to me and I would get up and go over to the stack of blankets and mattresses on the shelf and I would tuck the word in the middle of one of the banned books, between the cover of Shakespeare or Plato or Marx, and we would keep the words there, so that they would not be taken from us.

After my father lost his job as a fisherman he stopped bringing home the words with him. And why is it that, with tunnels so large we can haul cars and giraffes through them, why has my father never brought home a single word from his days working there? Certainly if a word can fit into a fishing net, it can fit through a tunnel. Or, is it possible that words—single words—are so large and dangerous to us, and them, that they too are part of the blockade?

⌒

I befriended the American in his first week in Jabaliya after I introduced him to my grandfather, Zajil. He would come to our house in block number five and listen to my grandfather's stories.

One late afternoon, the two of us were sitting along the wall drinking some mint tea. Other than an occasional child who came over to say hello, we were, for the most part, alone. Just down the street a scraggly-looking goat was rummaging through a bucket of watermelon rinds. The previous evening a man hauling a load of watermelon was passing up the street and Uncle Ali asked him how much he wanted for the watermelon. The driver of the cart told him the price of one, but Uncle Ali said he wanted to buy the entire cartload, about three dozen watermelons. The two men negotiated a price and soon everybody on School Street was eating watermelon.

I went over to the goat that was benefiting from our watermelon binge of the night before and began petting him. I took several almonds from my pocket and fed them to the goat.

"Have you ever seen a gazelle?" I asked the American.

"When I was a child, I went to a petting zoo once and I think there was a gazelle there; some kind of deer anyway."

"Did you pet it?"

"I think so. My parents took a photo of me with it. If I remember correctly, I was standing there, stiff as a board, about to cry."

"Why were you crying?"

"I guess I was afraid of it. I was four or five."

"I would love to pet a gazelle."

The conversation stalled and we went back to drinking our coffee. We watched the afternoon on School Street trudge by. Suddenly, the American began to speak.

"One day, a few years ago, I went to a homeless shelter to stay the night. I was going through some difficult times and wanted to see just how close I was to them. I stood in line until the shelter opened its doors. When *it came my turn to go inside, there was a man there who told me to strip down so he could delouse me. I have never felt so humiliated in my life."*

As I listened to him, it was as though I were listening to my grandfather telling me one of his stories up in the cemetery of the orange trees.

"Were you homeless?"

"No, I was one good friend away."

The American paused and took a sip of his now tepid coffee.

"Gaza reminds me of that night."

"How's that?"

"This place is one enormous wall built with the bricks of humiliation. When does it happen..." the American stopped.

"When does what happen?"

"That the dispossessed begin building walls?"

Across the way, atop a roof, several pigeons flapped their wings and cooed. One of the pigeons lost a gray-white feather and both of us watched its soft float all the way to the street.

⟋

One warm spring morning I took the American to the site where the train station in Gaza once stood. Nothing other than the skeleton of the platform remains. No rails. No ticket booth. No people. Nothing more than a ghost of the past, in this place teeming with ghosts.

I tell my friend the story of how, in that first winter in Gaza in 1948, the over 200,000 refugees were so desperate for firewood that they began to burn any and everything they could find: wooden toilet seats leftover from the British Mandate, trees, driftwood, and, lastly, they uprooted the railroad ties.

Before leaving, the American took a photo of me standing under the vacant, crumbling platform roof; I posed looking at my watch as if the train were late.

⟋

From a corner he watches several men, under the supervision of a band of soldiers, whitewash the painting of a red, black and green map from the wall. He is across the street when a soldier stares his way and begins walking toward him, slowly at first, then at a faster pace. The American remains where he is and in seconds the soldier is upon him, grabbing him by the shirt and shoving him backward. A second time he grabs a handful of shirt and pushes him further back, yelling at him in Hebrew, demanding his identification card.

He reaches into his back pocket and holds out his passport. Another soldier approaches, pushes aside his comrade and points him back across the way.

The soldier looks at the American and fingers through the document.

"I am sorry about that. We thought you were Palestinian." He returns the passport and walks away.

━

The moment that changes everything for him.

While sitting along School Street, playing backgammon with Bassam, a small boy stands before them. The boy holds an injured bird in his palm, a string tied around its neck. He throws the bird into the air where it flies a few feet before the string runs out and the bird is yanked downward.

In his notebook, the American writes—bird on a string. For the first time, he really begins to see Gaza. Begins to see himself.

━

That night, while everyone else is asleep, the American doesn't do so. Impossible to even try.

He thinks of his past years of darkness and how they pale to those of these people, but still, still it is his darkness and he has overcome it. He thinks to the boy with the bird on the string and he knows, more certain than anything he has ever known, that he has found, or it has found him, his life-work. These are the people and it is their stories, their stolen histories, their secrets, their tall tales that he must tell.

This is the greatest thing he can do, he thinks. This is the place he wants to be, but, he knows, achingly, that all over the world there are people like the Palestinians, and that he will not stay.

━

Border Shearing

One never forgets the first time they have their wool cut and the terror of it.

For me, the moment came five springs ago. I was in the sheepfold, the only home I had ever known, and it was the night before all of us lambs were to be shorn for the first time. There was a hum around the pens and I overheard several of the lambs talking of what awaited us the next morning. Our wool would be peeled from our bodies by one of the workers. The talk was how they would throw us on our backs and pin us down and take the shears and rip from us, in a single sheet, our wool. Relentlessly the lambs went on about how you didn't want Old Man Rashid to shear you. His beady eyes and the mouth, with its single tooth protruding like a tusk, made it all the worse as he glared down at you with those clippers buzzing like a disturbed hornet's nest. If you were unfortunate enough to get Old Man Rashid, the lambs continued, pinch your eyes tightly, until you see the white speckles dancing on your eyelids. I lay there wondering how those lambs knew so much of what was about to happen and yet I knew nothing. Perhaps their parents told them, I had thought, and since I had never known mine, that made all the sense.

That morning, the call to prayer startled the horizon and we, the lambs, were taken from the catching pen to the shearing stalls. We were lined up outside and one by one the lambs disappeared through a latch door and the insidious bleating stabbed the dawn and I searched for the man they spoke of the night before, looking for that single tooth and those eyes, but one worker seemed no different than the others.

While I was trying to locate the forewarned-about shearer, I was yanked by the back of my wool and thrown through one of those latch doors and when my eyes adjusted to the dim, dank room I saw a dozen Old Man Rashids, some with the heads of the horrified lambs in a stranglehold, others with heads pinned between the shearer's knees, but all the lambs had eyes bulging, like jelly, and in the beams of sunlight floated fluffs of the lambs' wool, reminding me of the summer before when I and my friends blew on the dandelions and we chased their seeds that wandered in the wind before they impregnated the fields. Gawking at my future, I thought of my promise to myself of the night before: that I would not cry, no matter how terrible it all was. But at that moment, my kept promise had nothing at all to do with bravery, or even the honor of keeping one's promise, but rather, it was fear itself that strangled my bawling deep in my gullet.

And then, with the same suddenness as when I had been heaved through the latch door, I was on my back and the shears had already begun plowing my virgin wool and I thought it was the morning coolness against my naked belly that I felt, but it was warm, and I imagined blood, the red of my blood against my white, white wool, but even worse than blood, I found that it was hot piss against my belly, which quickly turned into an icicle, a frigid spear of humiliation. And that, the humiliation, was worse than any pain I could imagine. The shearer worked over my belly, my back, each of my four legs, and under the chin. His sweat dripped and dribbled down upon my naked flesh and still I made not a sound; I think tears trundled from my eyes, but perhaps it was the fluids from him—how is one to know?

Within minutes I was flung out the opposite side of the shed and the sunlight sent prickles through my eyes. Before me, dozens of ridiculous-looking creatures stood, and I was nearly about to laugh or scream or cry when I realized that I was looking not only at them, but also myself.

⌒

Five years have passed and I am no longer a lamb, yet the feeling of the terror of those early years has resurfaced. It was only a week ago that one of the sheep had overheard some talk of how we would be taken away and sold. Not a few of us, but many.

No one dared speak of what was certainly on all our minds, that the end of Ramadan was only weeks away. Every year, as the holiday approaches, part of our flock disappears, never to be seen again. We know this, understand it to be our fate; that someday, in all likelihood, we will be chosen by a family, have our throats slit, and served for the feast of Eid. There is one hope, however, most of us share—that a good family, a family of stature, chooses us for their feast. Not the best of endings, perhaps, but still, dead is dead whether buried in a hole, or burned into ash, or churning at the bottom of one's stomach. For the most part, I believe that we sheep handle our mortality a hell of a lot better than humans.

What was being rumored was different, however. The talk was not of dozens, but of hundreds. Now, I don't want you to mistake me for some bitter old sheep, for I am not. I am just conveying, or trying to convey to you, the surprise at the large numbers that were being tossed around the grazing field that day.

And here we are, what was rumored has turned out to be truth.

They shove us onto the back of flatbed trucks, and they shove some more.

Legs and asses and heads and coats of wool everywhere, and the bed of the truck is slick with shit and sweat and bawling. But that is the *one* advantage of the crowdedness—when the weight in the truck shifts, and it often does, we are so close together that none of us really moves with it. The only advantage.

It takes much of the morning to load us onto the two flatbeds and then, northward, they drive. The sun is already high and hot and pummeling our backs and the tops of our heads. The bleak landscape of the Sinai is all-consuming. We are well beyond the central mountains that cast those elongated, mysterious and magical shadows; now all that is before us are flatlands, desert really, and for hours they are with us. By the time we near our destination, the sun is on the right side of our faces, low, allowing the slats on the side of the truck to provide us with a strip of warm shade.

It is night before we arrive, a mile from the border. They will not allow us off the trucks, afraid, I guess, that we will flee, the hundreds upon hundreds of us would scatter in a hundred different directions. But that just shows how little they truly know about us; we gather in flocks and rarely stray on our own, going to where the food is, except, of course, for a few black sheep, and who really gives a damn about them, that minuscule minority that exists in all walks and tribes and races of life.

Left to stand throughout the night, we shift from hoof to hoof in order to give brief moments of relief to one of our legs and also to try to keep warm on this night that has started out cold and only grows colder. Crammed together as we are brings little warmth. My face is pressed into the side of another sheep and I raise my head to gasp a breath of the night air. Quickly my neck and jaw lock into the vice of a cramp and I must lower my head to relieve the pain.

I begin to call out the names of friends, hoping to find at least one of them nearby so that we may talk away the drudgery of the stars. Name after name I loft into the night—*J* and *D* and *M*. The only answer—angry words:

"Shut the hell up with all your selfish prattle," yells an elder sheep. "We are all in the same situation and yet you think of only yourself!"

Ignoring the harsh words I continue until, at last, *M*, lets out a shout.

"K-02, is that you?"

"Yes, it is. You're M-02?" I ask, referring to his letter and year he was born.

"Yes, it's me. I'm on the opposite side of the truck."

"Do you know where we are?"

"A couple of the sheep said we are at the Gaza border."

"Gaza? What are we doing there?"

"That's only what I heard."

"Why is it so cold?"

"It's March..."

"Shush, you bleating idiots!" interrupts the elder sheep. "Gaza, Egypt, what does it matter?" His laugh gurgles into the night.

"A simple sweep with their knives will leave you bleating no more."

I dare not speak, afraid to ruffle, even more, the ire of the elder sheep. A sudden, vicious shiver jolts me. I want nothing more than for the sun to rise and for them to let us off this truck, leaving us to whatever our destiny may hold.

—

And the sun does come up, grudgingly, but up. The back of the flatbeds bang open and all the sheep push and trample one another in their scurry to get off. What's the hurry, I think, but I shoo that thought away, for I spent the night thinking of little else.

My legs are beyond feeling; even the pain has somehow gone away, or at least it cowers somewhere. As I am about to jump off the back of the truck, my legs give way, splaying in all directions, and I fall, hard, to the ground. Stunned, I lie there, the blue dome of the sky above me, the tan dirt beneath. One man tries to lift me, but I am difficult to move. A second man prods me with a toe of his boot; I feel it against my ribs, but there is not pain, merely a dull nudge. I make it to my feet and nearly collapse again. I am dizzy and when I look and see the beautiful azure blue ahead of me, as well as above, I am disconcerted. Looking down, the ground is at my hooves, where it should be, but the blue also seems to be at my feet as well, although distant. Then, the air holds the answer—the sea, of course, we are near the sea.

In all my distraction, the others have been herded off; my fellow sheep are a swelling cloud of white rustling the dust like a storm, away from the border, departing. Only a few sheep are near me, none of whom I recognize. I want to catch up and find my friends, particularly M-02, but the two men are flailing us back with sticks. They turn us around, away from the moving flock, and push us past the trucks toward the border.

Shouts and shots erupt behind me, and when I turn to look, one of the men whacks me with the stick and is about to hit me again, but somehow I manage to get a little life into my legs and scamper out of reach. More gunshots and the commotion swells. Suddenly, appearing before me, like a gopher popping out of a hole, is a man, soiled in reddish clay. His dirty hands reach out to me, and I try to avoid them, but I am shoved from behind and once again my legs are failing me and the dirty man has me in a stranglehold; at first, I think, stupidly, that he is about to shear me, but before I know it I am face-first in an enormous esophagus, the same color that covers the man.

᠊᠊᠊

Nothing, there is nothing that distresses me more than tight, enclosed spaces. At least on the back of the truck, crowded though it was, there was no roof and the open sky allowed us a little space. Not even the clipping of my hooves comes close to evoking this terror of enclosed spaces, although, I must admit, when the shearer grips the clippers in one hand, my leg in the other, my heart pitter-patters a bit. That all stems from a single incident, a couple of years back, when my front left hoof was cut too close and became infected. The infection worsened; so debilitated was I, that there was talk that they might put me to sleep, the sleep where one doesn't awaken. This tunnel is far worse than any infection.

As I fall, my front hooves dig into a side of the tunnel opening and rather than slow my fall, I become stuck, wedged, more like it, with my head on one side of the tunnel, my rear on the other. My legs are left dangling, flailing away as though I had been tossed into the Great Sea itself. But instead of water, my legs kick wildly at air. I can only imagine the sight I must be. Those wild spindly legs of mine and my head and ass stuck, all the while sound is blurred—if it is possible for sound to be blurry—like being underwater, I guess. Again, my imagination at work here, for I have never been within a mile of the sea, although once, while at the drinking trough, a rambunctious herder dunked my head underwater and held it there and the voices and the tussling of the wind in the trees and my booming heart all were garbled.

Somehow I wriggle free in the tunnel opening and drop the remaining eight or ten feet to the floor. Landing on my side, I look up to see the man who pushed me down here, stepping two rungs at a time, on a ladder of sorts, something, of course, I cannot do. Each step draws protests from the rungs. Chunks of dirt fall and I turn my head away. Then his feet, without shoes, are against me.

"Get moving. We have a long way to crawl, my fat little friend."

I lift my head and go onto all fours, but must stoop, for my back and head bang against the roof. It is difficult to move, too narrow to even turn my head and try shaking out the pieces of moist clay that fall into my ears. The man relentlessly prods me with a stick and I am tired of it and release a fart, long and sorrowful, into his face. Back off, it shouts!

I hurry as best I can to escape the smell and now, at least, there is a little distance between the man, his stick and me.

There is a dim light in the tunnel and every once in a while, an air vent. My breathing comes in choppy, hysteric gasps. I see no light at the end of the tunnel and a panic overcomes me and I turn, barely able to do so in the narrowness, but I manage to run, as best I can, directly at the man, all the while my back scraping against the roof and I gather no speed, but I do catch him off guard. I lower my head and ram into his groin and he lets out a groan and falls backward. As I am about to crawl over him, he grabs my leg and I think it will snap and I begin to thrash at him with my hooves, which, if you have never met a sheep before, you should be aware that our hooves are quite heavy and sharp. But the man doesn't let go and I don't stop kicking and we battle on until I feel a large block of dirt drop on my back.

"You idiot sheep; you're going to get the both of us killed!"

The struggle continues and my breath is hard to come by.

"Tunnel collapse!" he yells, letting go of my leg.

I scramble back over him and a muffled cry I hear and then only my breathing thrumming through my ears. I turn my head and see nothing but dirt and on the floor is the man's walkie-talkie. I continue in the same direction, thinking that, surely, I must be underneath Gaza by now.

Never have I had a great sense of time, so I am not certain how long it has taken me to get through the tunnel. It could be an hour later or a day. I drop when I reach the end, where there is a thirty-foot high shaft, above which is a blue square of the bluest sky I have ever seen. Too tired to make a sound, I wait until someone looks down into the shaft. Behind me, I listen for the man, but know that he will not emerge, at least not from this end of the tunnel.

More time goes by; I may have fallen into a nap and I hear voices and when I look up there are faces staring down at me. One man yells something and I am too tired to budge or to make a sound. Seconds later a stream of cold water splatters atop me; startled, I jump, hitting my head for the millionth time on the roof. I let out a halfhearted bleat or baah, whatever, it probably isn't strong enough for anyone to hear and what would it matter anyway?

A man is making his way down the ladder and grabs hold of me, tying a harness around my body. He shouts to the faces looking down.

"Mahmoud is not here!"

"Can you see him in the tunnel?"

"No. Try his walkie-talkie."

The man tightens the harness around me; it is digging into my belly, but I do not protest or bite his calf or thigh.

"Lift up!" the man shouts. "I am going to take a look."

Suddenly I am off my feet and in the air going up through the shaft. The harness has a stranglehold on me; my breath is cut off. I dare not look down, for heights are not a thing I enjoy, and already a wave of nausea swells. Above me the hole grows, as do the faces, silhouetted by the sky. Near the top, two pairs of hands grab and pull me out and remove the harness. I stagger and throw up onto the ground. No one pays me any attention, for which I am most grateful. I hear the crackle of a radio and the men are talking into their phones. One man begins to yell for the others to come and help, there has been a collapse inside the tunnel and there is no answer from Mahmoud. One by one several of the men disappear into the shaft, while a growing number of others clamor around its mouth.

⚊

Slowly, trying not to draw any attention, I begin to walk away from the people gathering around the entrance of the tunnel. No one looks, or if they do, it is halfhearted. I continue at the same pace, a saunter that is not unusual for sheep. Imagine you are watching a sheep walking through a sparse field and how he stops whenever he finds something to chew on. That is me, nosing around, but also very much aware of getting further and further from the tunnels.

Behind me, a man approaches quickly; I stop, trying to act as casual as possible. He hurries past. I see him holding a young girl, her head resting on his shoulder. I see her face, a beautiful, sad face, with eyes the color and shape of dates, encased by a light pink headscarf. She is crying, that much I can tell, and our eyes meet and we hold them and there is so much sadness and confusion in those eyes, larger and even more prominent because of the tiny ponds of tears. And I wonder if she can see the tears in my eyes—from where they come, I do not know—and can she hear them plopping into the parched dust of Gaza, and if she can, what is it she hears?

⁒

No one stops me and I walk. I am hungry and come upon a fallen, limp carrot in an alleyway and gnaw on it. Against the base of a small tree, I try to rub the tunnel dirt from my nostrils, but it only pushes it further inside, and with each breath I taste the soil.

No longer am I in the city of Rafah, but the refugee camp of the same name. Cement block houses are everywhere. The alleyways are tight. I pass a cart, and the donkey pulling it turns and smirks at me. So typical of a donkey, I think, smirking at a sheep. To be honest, I have never much cared for donkeys and how they so often seem to be looking down at us. And why is that? Is it because they are laborers and they look at us as lazy animals? Well, I ask, how many donkeys have provided a man with a warm coat in winter?

I continue down the street until coming upon a school, and behind it, a couple of trees. To there I go and drop to the ground and rest my long-open eyes, too tired to even give a thought to the hundreds of my fellow sheep on the other side of the border.

⁒

I sleep down along the beach, sometimes on the sand itself, but usually not, for the fleas have taken a liking to burrowing in my wool and nipping away at me. I am in desperate need to be shorn; the heat, although it is only May, is stifling. Other than in an alleyway, there is little shade in this city of Gaza, a place I stay away from during the day because I only attract attention. Late nights, however, I do find myself out foraging through the streets for food. Remarkable how quickly I have adapted to being more nocturnal; a few short weeks and I have nearly become an owl.

Most days, I see other animals: donkeys, of course, some birds, mainly seagulls and pigeons, both of which seem no different than those I saw in Egypt. And one night, although I cannot be for certain, I heard what I thought to be a lion of some kind, and on that same night, closer to dawn, a high-pitched mewing of a peacock. I am not convinced of the lion, but I am certain that I heard a peacock, or something else like it, unbelievable as that may sound. Back in Egypt, there were several of them, for some reason, in the sheepfold.

I do dream, and they are quite vivid at times, but this was not a dream. I was sleeping that night under an abandoned fishing boat and when I heard the peacock I stood up and started to follow the sound to where I thought it was coming from. But when I began to walk in the direction of the city, away from the echoing bend of the sea, I could not be sure from what direction the sound of the peacock came.

And on this morning I hear it again. It must be mating season, I think. I walk along the coastal road, which I have become familiar with. Once, I took it two miles, northward, ending up in Beach Camp, a sprawl, where I found some tasty offerings for dinner. I head there on this morning; daytime I feel more comfortable in the camps, where there are the always-present goats, with which I can somewhat blend in.

It is early, but the sun has begun to blush the eastern sky. This is the time I love most, and even more since I have been on my own. I do a lot of walking, but it is difficult; the sand is slow going and the streets wear at my hooves. I am in no hurry and keep to the road. Behind me, I hear the clacking of hooves; much faster than mine. Soon, next to me is a tired, old horse, without a harness or a cart behind it like most horses in Gaza, tired-looking or not. He is the first to talk.

"I've seen you around here a couple of times."

"Possibly," I try, faking surprise.

"No, for certain."

I stare at his huge eyes, the eyelashes of which are long and soft looking. He is a big horse, probably at one time powerful, but now, as I have said, tired, and not just tired from a sleepless night or two, but from a hard life, one of hauling heavy loads day in and day out, until, finally, he just quit.

"Maybe I have been here a while."

"Not maybe, for sure. And you are not from around here, but, most likely, from Egypt."

A stubborn thing, this here horse; must have a donkey as a father. My ears twitch at his words.

"I'm correct."

"How can you tell?"

"It is the reddish dirt on you. That only comes from the tunnels and they, of course, are only on the Egyptian side of the border."

I say nothing and look away.

"There is no reason to hide the fact; the tunnels are certainly no secret. Half the people you see here work there in some way or other. A growing number even die there."

What does he know, I wonder? I walk a little faster, but he keeps up.

"Almost all of the animals in the zoo come through the tunnels."

"Zoo?"

"Yes, we have several zoos here, but the main one is about a mile away, in the Bureij district of the city. You should give it a look. They could probably use a sheep without a home."

"Is there a peacock there?"

"Two, in fact. Brought them all the way from Asia, I guess."

"I thought I heard one this morning, but was surprised."

"Noisy animals, and they only scream at night. Always calling attention to themselves."

"Why do they have a zoo here?"

"For the kids, mostly. There is not much in the way of beauty or peacefulness in this place; in case you haven't noticed."

"The sea is beautiful," I say, pointing my nose in the direction of the water.

"Yes, but only if you don't think about what is at your back."

"What other animals do they have in the zoo?"

"A gazelle, mountain lions, the peacocks that I mentioned, camels, monkeys, even a giraffe."

"How the hell did they get a giraffe through the tunnels?"

"Good question. Even an occasional miracle, I guess, graces Gaza."

"Are there no sheep?"

"Not that I know of. Certainly not one of your color!" The horse shows his huge teeth as he chuckles.

"Yes, I know that I could use a shearing."

"And a bath."

"You are quite blunt with your words."

"Not many words left in this old mouth. Use them while I still can."

⚊

I sleep for a while near Beach Camp, then, about an hour before dawn I walk to the neighborhood where the zoo is. Although it is quiet, I do see a couple of people out in the streets, one, a man with large rubber boots, more than likely a fisherman or a worker in the fish market, another, an old man huddled under a burlap sack, sleeping atop a cart.

I can smell the zoo before coming upon it. A strange, intoxicating blend of odors, some of which I recognize, of course—the camels and birds—the others I can only imagine.

As I near the zoo, with its brick entrance and black gates, a peacock begins to stir and its scream lacerates the approaching dawn. The peacock continues mewing, louder and louder, and a squeal of a monkey, a growl from a lion, a grunting giraffe join in the discord. Startled, and in a rush to get out of there, my hooves gain little traction on the gray bricks, but finally I begin to run in the direction of the sea. Slipping around a corner, I slide into the arms of two men, both dressed in black and white-striped sweaters. Men dressed as zebras. They wrestle me to the ground and one of them, within seconds, has my feet roped together. My bleating joins in the discordant choir and it continues until I have not a single syllable left inside my throat.

⚊

They have taken me inside a large room and lay me on the floor. My feet are still tied. One of the men has a knife in his hand and I think; so, this is your fate, this is how all sheep feel as the knife, not as glistening as I imagined it would be, dirty in fact, makes its descent.

I have heard that one's life will flash before them, tiny pictures making a quilt of your history. Nothing like that happens at all. The knife is near and passes my throat and belly and with one quick swipe the rope is severed and my legs, as though springs, snap open. I want to jump up and race around the room and celebrate my freedom, my continuation of life, but I cannot move. Cannot so much as wiggle an ear.

"What an interesting color we have here. We are certainly the only zoo in Gaza to have a red sheep. Imagine how the children will love him!"

"Stand up, my friend. Let's see the whole of you." The taller of the two men comes over and tries to lift me, but I am deadweight.

"Help me, Farid. He's a heavy one."

Farid puts his hands under me and together they lift. I do not help them in any way, keeping my body as limp as possible, but I can resist no longer, besides, the tall man's fingers dig into my belly, tickling me.

I stand before them.

They walk circles around me.

Sometimes they touch me, looking inside and behind my ears, at my teeth, raising my legs and checking my hooves. I allow them to do with me what they wish. They comment on my matted wool, the color of it, the need for my hooves to be clipped. Then they walk out of the room and I am left standing in the middle. One of the men, reaching back through a crack in the door, flips off the light; I still don't budge in the darkness and I am standing where the men left me when the door opens, the light comes back, and the men, along with a veterinarian, enter.

— ~ —

With great care, the vet shears my wool while the men watch. He doesn't nick me, not a drip of my blood dots the floor. Although my hooves haven't been trimmed for some time, they are not that bad for I have walked a lot and the cement of the coastal road, and in the city itself, have worn them. When finished, the vet sticks me with a needle; even that is done with care. Where, I wonder, has this man been all these years? I walk around the room, shiver, not because I am cold, but rather a sudden chill has trundled down my back. I feel so light and clean without my wool. Because of the vet, my first day in the Gaza Zoo is bearable.

— ~ —

For the next several weeks of sunrises I remain in the room, where they feed me twice a day and allow time for my wool to grow. I have not seen the vet since that first morning. One day both men come into the room and I go over to them, thinking I will be fed, but they have no food, only a small bucket with a reddish-brown liquid in it. One of the men takes hold of me, and for the first time since they brandished the knife, I feel a runnel of fear.

The other man, Farid, wears long, orange rubber gloves, up to the biceps; he is the one holding the bucket. The man steadying me in place whispers in my ear to stay calm, nothing bad is going to happen, but it is his whispers that make me all the more anxious. Like with the man in the tunnel, seemingly years ago, I begin to flail and a struggle ensues. Farid places the bucket on the floor and helps his friend try to contain me, but I elude them and lunge for and kick the bucket, sending the red liquid across the floor and splatting the gray walls.

They look at me with surprise more than anger. Farid picks up the bucket, ignoring the mess and they leave the room and do not return until late that night and Shafiq, the veterinarian, is with them and he gives me a little pinprick on the rear and I slip into sleep and waken to see a red-woolen sheep, me, the color of the tunnel.

It is on my second night in the pen that the first animal speaks to me. We, the smaller, cloven-footed animals are housed in a pen, surrounded by a large metal fence, rather than a cage. We have room to walk. This silence is as much my doing as theirs. Mostly, for me, I am embarrassed and uncomfortable about the way I look and I stay in the far-right corner, away from the others. It is in this corner that I keep to at night and in this corner that a soft voice speaks to me, a voice so soft that I think it is whispering because of the hour.

It turns out that the voice is always this soft.

"I haven't had a chance to say hello and welcome you to the zoo."

"Why would you welcome anyone to a place where they are not free to leave?"

"I was also not too happy to be here, but it isn't such a bad place. Anyway, I just came to say hello."

The small tapping of hooves I listen to as the animal turns and walks away, soft, the steps, like the voice. I am about to tell him to stop and come back, but I say nothing and the steps fade into the night.

—

It is the day before the beginning of summer vacation, when the school children will begin to visit in larger numbers. I make myself as inconspicuous as possible and try to figure out who the unseen pen-mate was that I spoke with last night. There are not that many possibilities, I figure. Judging by the voice alone, I quickly eliminate the two cows and the giraffe; whoever heard of a cow or a giraffe with a gentle, soft voice? Even more so, whoever heard of a cow or giraffe walking with such quiet steps? I admit that I have never met a giraffe before, but common sense tells me that an animal that large cannot walk or speak as softly as what I heard last night. Now, I have known a few cows, and can say with almost certainty that it was no cow that approached me last night.

By mid-morning, the choice is narrowed to the goat or the gazelle. Closing my eyes, I imagine each of them speaking to me, the words I remember clearly, the tone, the breaths during the pauses. The thing that convinces me it is the gazelle is that the goat has a nearly white coat, and at night, even in a night as dark as last, I would have seen at least a hint of it. Besides, only those tiny black hooves of the gazelle could walk, glide is the better word, like that. Glorious hooves, shiny, despite the dirt—coffee beans at the bottom of the fragile legs. That is why they can run so fast, I think, making up for their lack of strength. They are an animal that avoids confrontation, peaceful creatures, I imagine.

Once or twice during the afternoon, I catch myself gazing at the gazelle, one of the most beautiful, lithe animals I have ever seen. Although I want to go over and talk to him, I hesitate, not only because the zookeepers discourage us gathering during the day, but also for the simple fact that I was rude the night before.

So, I wait and watch as the sheet of dusk becomes a thick shroud over the zoo. I keep my eye on the gazelle to see where he stays during the night and then go over there a little while after I hear the diminishing of the usual night chatter.

Cautiously I make my way across the ground to where the gazelle is. I try to walk as quietly as possible, but I am not much better than my fellow, heavy-hooved animals.

"You have decided to talk to me." The silky voice of last night guides me the final ten yards.

"I was just walking around before going off to sleep."

"Yes, sometimes I like to do that as well. But starting tomorrow, with the larger crowds, I rarely have the desire to do so at night. Eat and then sleep; that is the repetition of summer."

"I hear that the days are long."

"That they are and the children love to pet us, and there are always those that like to tease, and the rare few who enjoy tormenting us."

"I am not looking forward to that."

"None of us are, but at least we have the nights, for the most part, to ourselves. For me, that is the one beauty of not being in a cage."

"But those in the cages can at least hide and rest during the days, if they so choose."

"I imagine, but if there are too many complaints about not seeing the monkeys or the birds, the zookeepers force them to come out into the open."

I yawn and the gazelle echoes it.

"Well, I am tired and should get back to my place. Anyway, it was good talking to you, and I apologize for being so rude last night."

"Apology accepted. See you bright and early."

"Bright and early."

⌐

And before the sun has time to broil the air, they have arrived. Many, as I have been told, head first to the monkey cages, always the most popular. The monkeys are fifty yards away and yet I can hear the laughter of the children. How wonderful, I think, being able to make children laugh. I look over at the gazelle. The low-sitting sun brings out the two black stripes on his white face, his stripes, the gorgeous, subtle tones appear as though they have been painted there with the simplest sweep of a brush. Unlike my coat, his was done by the brush-stroke of nature.

In time, the children make it to the petting area and the gate is opened by one of the workers, who promptly shuts it after the children enter, in order that none of us escape, something that is a rarity, but it did happen once last winter, I have heard, when a goat raced through a gate left open. A cluster of children head to the gazelle, squealing at its cuteness, but one girl, wearing a blue school dress like the rest, spots me and comes in my direction. Startled, I run away from her and she chases me, which attracts the attention of some of the others and they too are in full pursuit and soon I tire and one of the zookeepers has ahold of me and keeps me there, talking calmly, while one of the girls comes and rubs my red head and the man tells her to touch me nicely, and she does. The other girls follow suit—gently, the zookeeper says—and they do as well and I am surprised that their hands feel rather nice and once, even, I close my eyes.

I'm not sure what to do or how to act when the children pet me; I have been told nothing. Watching the girls go over to the gazelle, I see that feeding us is not permitted, for one of the zookeepers points to the sign when a girl tries giving the gazelle a piece of candy. Speaking of candy—I hate it. Not that anyone has tried feeding me any, but that it is sticky and when they touch me with those hands it gets caught all up in my wool and other kids, with their dirty hands, touch me, and in no time my red wool becomes matted and often it hurts when I walk or lie down because it pulls at and pinches my skin.

By the end of the day, actually, well before the zoo closes, I have had enough and I am so tired of it all that I don't even care to be cleaned or to eat; I just want to drop to my corner of the pen and sleep the stars away. But even then, sleep does not come easily. I am distracted by dreams, nightmares even, where every time I begin to relax a child comes up and begins petting me or someone snaps a photo, which leaves tiny galaxies on the inside of my eyelids and they bob there, not allowing me the rest that I need before it all begins again in a few short hours.

Never could I have imagined how exhausting it is to have children pay attention to you all day.

Tonight, a sultry night, an hour after we have been hosed down, I am unable to fall asleep and I make my way to where the gazelle stays and he is awake so we talk a little.

"Trouble sleeping?"

"How did you know?"

"It happens to all of us in our first weeks here."

"Do you have any suggestions?"

"Embrace the dreams."

"Embrace them? They won't allow me any rest."

"That's because you are fighting them. When the children won't let you alone and they pet you until you think your fur will fall off, imagine they are petting you on the spot that makes you feel good and relaxed and calm."

"I can't imagine that working."

"Teach yourself how to imagine this. If not, you will go crazy in here. Lie down for a minute."

I do as the gazelle says and he takes his front hooves, those tiny hooves that seem so fragile, but are surprisingly strong, and he rubs the lower part of my head, where the skull meets the back.

"Think of the children's hands, clean and gentle, and there is no shrill in their voices, only calmness, matching the stroke of their fingers. Over and over they touch you and it relaxes you and your warm eyelids drift over your tired eyes."

That is the last thing I hear and I wake up and for the first time since I came here I feel refreshed and ready for another day.

―

So, too, are the patrons tired at the end of the day: the giggling of the children becomes less and less; they rub their tired eyes; running is almost non-existent. All around the zoo the voices grow weaker and I listen until they dwindle into their cars or, if walking, their fading footsteps as they head to houses somewhere in the city. I have grown to love this time of night, before we are hosed down and fed and left alone until morning. Some nights I eat with the gazelle and we talk until sleep comes upon us. My nightmares have lessened, although they sometimes occur, but mostly I am able to wake myself before they get too far along and I walk around until my tiredness blots out the bad dream. The zoo is calm at night, except for the occasional mewing of the peacocks, which happens not as often, now that the mating season has passed.

Even though there are many animals I have never met, at least I know all in my pen and I have begun to feel more comfortable in here. In addition to the gazelle, there are other cloven-hooved animals with us—a couple of goats, a white donkey, two cows, a giraffe and a pregnant camel. All, except for the donkey, which I have told you that I don't care for the species, talk with me. I don't mean that the two of us never talk, for we do, but there is always this distance between us and the talk is mainly in passing.

For the most part all of us are too busy to speak much and, at night, too exhausted. When we do speak, it is normal animal chitchat, not so different than you can hear anywhere: the lack of taste with the food; the fascination of some children's need to play with our ears; the best remedy for a split hoof; of our lives before we came through the man-made tunnels—that one commonality that so many of us share. It is when we begin to speak of our prior lives that the conversations tend to drift into the night and a silence ensues and each of us is alone with our thoughts, and if the wind is just right, we can sometimes hear the repetition of the sea.

Before we know it, the six weeks of summer vacation is about over and soon our afternoons will begin to slow down, although some groups of children will be brought in on class trips. The days are hot, but at night there is a hint of the slightly cooling days of September. In Gaza, summer is a struggle for autumn to fight off, the season so short, as if it were exhausted from the heat and the fight, that it just lies down and allows winter to traipse over it.

The gazelle and one of the goats are talking with me while we savor the occasional breeze. Never one to hold back his words, the goat says:

"Why is it that our friend the donkey doesn't like you much?"

Surprised by the question, I pause, not sure what to say, and the gazelle, in his soft voice, answers before I can manage to come up with something.

"He's jealous of the color of your wool and how the children have taken a liking to you. The problem with him, and any donkey that has been in here, is that he is no different than what the children see in their daily lives, so they pay him very little attention. That's difficult for any animal to take."

"Jealous of my wool! Why would anyone be jealous of this red blanket?"

The goat looks at me.

"Because it's different," he answers.

"Different doesn't make it good."

"I never said that. But different is different. Instead of closing your eyes when the people are petting you, you should start paying more attention. The people who come here are even more trapped than us. The one beautiful thing about this place is that we offer these people something a little different in their lives. Anything that is at all different is good for them—even if it, like you, looks like a big fuzzy apple." The goat snickers and his straggly beard quivers a little.

Despite the goat's utter lack of humor, I am surprised by his observations. I have never thought that goats were all that intelligent, not much more than a donkey, but, at least this one here I will look at differently from now on.

I notice that the gazelle is not paying attention to our banter. I turn my head to look at what he is engrossed in. The goat turns and what we all see is the donkey, the donkey we were just speaking of, being led out through the gate.

"Where do you think they are taking him?" I ask.

"Probably for his shots. It is about that time," answers the gazelle.

The gate closes with a squeak and I say good night to my friends and head to the opposite end of the pen to sleep.

―

I enjoy the slowing days, but they are short-lived because, by the end of the week, we have a new addition to the petting pen. With much fanfare, a zebra has been brought in, a boon for us, for we are the only zoo in all the Gaza Strip to have one. It was smuggled through the tunnels, at great expense, I hear. Attendance grows to nearly summer levels. There is also a buzz around the cages and petting pen as well. They have made a special area for the zebra, where even we in the petting pen cannot get too close to him. I have seen him from afar and the black and white of its stripes nearly glow. The pen where they keep the zebra is packed with not only awestruck children but many adults as well. With the overflow at the zebra pen, some of the crowd is moved into our area where they pay us scant attention and, for the most part, we are little more than a waiting area until the zebra admirers thin out.

I am over near the zebra's pen, trying to get a better look at him myself, when a young schoolgirl in a headscarf comes over and begins to pet me. I am still trying to get a glimpse of the zebra while her hand remains on the top of my head and down my back. Top of my head and down my back. The repetition is soothing and I forget about the zebra and shut my eyes. Again and again she pets me and even when her friends call out her name—Haneen, they yell, Haneen, coaxing her to come over to the zebra—even then her hand stays on me. Not until she drops her small schoolbag do I open my eyes, and as she bends to pick it up we look at one another. Immediately I recognize her, remember the smell of her as she passed that day, in the arms of the man carrying her away from the tunnels. How many months has it been? With my red wool, I'm hoping she doesn't recognize me.

But she does. Although there is nowhere for me to go, I run away, but unlike the children that first day in the zoo, she doesn't pursue me, rather, she stands and watches me get as far away from her as possible. I am not certain how long she stands there, for I keep my face burrowed in the corner, beneath the tree where I sometimes go to get out from under the beating summer sun. But the hours have passed and there is no sun now, only the moon, scaling the sky, full and bright.

⌐

With the moon at its brightest and the zoo asleep, tonight is a good night to go over to the zebra's pen and try to get a look at him. It has been a long, traumatic day, with me seeing the girl and all. Her image pesters me, and even though I have seen her in a different light, still, it is that crying face of hers, minutes after I made it through the tunnel, that is emblazoned in my head.

The zebra's pen has bars so close together that I can barely poke my face through them. With the moon past its apex and dropping toward the horizon, the zebra is easy to see; its white stripes—or is it that the stripes are black—never mind, the white glows in the moonlight. I wedge my face between the bars a little more in order to get a better angle, a better look. The zebra, about twenty yards away, stirs in its sleep and turns its head toward me.

"Who are you?" it asks. "What are you doing here?"

Startled, I try to free my face from between the bars, but can't. I am stuck. Bracing my front hooves against the bottom of the pen, I pull and twist yet still my face is imprisoned.

The zebra stands and again asks the same question. This time the voice sounds deeper than I imagine a zebra's voice should be, although I have never met one before. I try to answer, but my mouth and jaws can barely open and a long, drawn out, somewhat trembling *sheep* creeps into the night's quiet. The zebra approaches and is within a foot of me before speaking.

"Well, well, if isn't my furry red friend."

I know that voice, not a zebra, but a donkey.

"That's where you've been." The words hurt coming out.

"What, you thought that you would always be the only newly created animal in this place?"

"Help me," I manage.

He flashes me that arrogant look that I despise. Stripes or no stripes, he is still a donkey.

"If I do help you, you must promise that you will tell no one. Never spoil, for the children, the secret of the only zebra in Gaza. Or, maybe I will just go back to sleep and they will discover your pinched, red face in my pen. Maybe you will stay there until you become thin enough to free your face."

The painted donkey turns and takes a step, then glares at me.

"Promise," I say.

He lifts his ridiculous donkey ear.

"Promise," I repeat.

He gets real close and his breath stinks. Again, that smirk. He turns and I think he is going to leave me there, when suddenly, without warning, he raises his legs and kicks me in the nose and I fly backwards, free of the pen, the whole of the night zoo swimming in my tears, and I see him strutting away until the glowing white of his body fades into the black of his fake stripes.

I wake in a bright, unnatural light, the echoing squawk of the words—*Thank you... thank you... thank you...* interspersed with an occasional *Have a nice day... have a nice day.*

In addition to the high-pitched squawking, there is a human's voice and the words are mimicked and each time they pummel my head. My eyes creak open and through the thin gauze that wraps my head, I see two birdcages hanging from the ceiling of the room, the same room where they held me in my first days in the zoo. Standing beneath the cages is Shafiq, the veterinarian, and when he hears me stir, he comes over.

"How is our little friend today?"

"Have a nice day, have a nice day," the parrots mimic.

He turns and laughs at the green birds.

"Animals that talk. Isn't that amazing!" His attention returns to me.

Yes, I think, utterly amazing. His face is next to mine, so close that when I look at him my eyes cross, making my head feel as though it is being kicked over and over.

"You took quite a hit there, didn't you?"

A kick, I think, yes I took quite a kick by that damn fraud of a beast that you have in here. The vet pulls back a little and I can see him more clearly. He is wearing glasses that make his eyes real big, like those of a fish or something. He looks me over.

"You could use a shearing and a new coloring."

It's about time you notice that, I think, but little good that will do, summer is over and winter is coming and that is when I need the coat.

As though he reads my mind, the vet answers.

"Maybe just a new coloring, then we can shear you in spring."

With those words, he leaves the room. I close my eyes and the parrots babble on, each screech a stick against the drum of my head.

I am back in the zoo, my growing re-dyed red wool a calendar for all of us in the petting pen. I have not been sheared since I came here and the wool is more than four inches thick. I should be warm this winter and, for that, I am grateful.

The parrots are also here, over by the peacock, and they and their sparse vocabulary are the new buzz at the zoo. The zebra continues to be a popular attraction, but only after the patrons *ooooh* and *aaaaah* at the speaking birds. They try to get them to say other words and phrases, but the birds seem incapable of repeating anything other than *thank you* and *have a nice day*. Still, for now, the customers are seemingly satisfied with this. These birds rarely seem to sleep and my dreams are filled with thoughts of going over there and rattling their cages until they say *thank you* never again.

I avoid the zebra pen, although, from a distance, we catch an occasional glimpse of one another. I must admit that I am a little jealous of the fake zebra. At times, I want to shout to the children that the zebra is a fraud, it is just a damn, stupid donkey, no different than those they see every day pulling carts loaded with watermelon or trash or wood.

For the most part I keep to myself because my headaches persist, but also I simply do not care to talk to any of them. The gazelle has tried speaking to me. A couple of times he has come over to my side of the pen, under the tree, but I tell him that my head hurts, which it does, but I am afraid that I will break my promise to the zebra, although, after what he did to me I really don't give a damn what happens. But, a promise is a promise, and what good are they if you can't keep them?

⸝

We all have moments in our lives where we will never forget the sounds and the odors and the taste of bile in our wretched throats when we witness something, something perhaps we could have prevented or at least altered in some small way. But we do nothing and we have a scroll of excuses as to why not. Loathing. Jealousy. Weakness. Indifference. It doesn't matter in the least if all of them are true, or parts of each, or even just a sliver of one. What matters is that we did nothing.

As I lie in the stunned Gaza dawn I think not of the horror that has just passed, perhaps it is all too close, both personally and in time, but what I can't erase from my mind is the sunset of the night before, that bloody mole on the forehead of the horizon. As that sun hit the sea, you could almost hear it sizzling, and instead of disappearing in an orb-shape, as it almost always does, it began to flatten out, and although I couldn't see it all from the zoo, I am certain that the water and caps of the waves were red, and when they hit and rushed upon the shore, they stained the sand with their blood, this shore that has seen its litany of bloody sand: Alexander the Great; Bishop Porphyry; Napoleon; 1948. Much more sadness than any shore should have to bear.

I am sleeping when the parrots begin their jabber. Unusual for them, these bright green birds, who normally talk themselves to sleep. Even a month after being kicked by the zebra, my headaches continue and the high-pitched voices of the parrots are knives. I stand and walk from behind the tree that I have claimed as mine. Groggily, I go over toward the zebra pen, as close that I have been since the last full moon, which, on this night, is nearly so again. How I wish that there was never a moon, that all nights were sheathed in buzzard-black.

I am close enough to the zebra's pen to see that he, too, is awake and standing on the far side looking in the direction of the parrots. I see his tail swishing back and forth. Once, he shivers his head as though an icy hand is slithering down his back. I hear, as does he, the frantic screeches of the parrots getting closer. Snow fills my veins.

At first I don't see the men. Their black masks and pants and shirts and boots conceal them, but their white eyes give them away. The more I stare, the clearer their figures become. One of the men holds the parrots' cage, two others have guns and they shoot bang, bang the lock on the zebra's pen. The man with the parrots stays outside while those with the guns stride toward the zebra. One of them unleashes what I think is a chain, but I hear no clinking, and realize it is a rope. He lassoes the neck of the donkey and, at first, as if he could not believe what is happening to him, the donkey stands passive, solemn almost. But when the rope tightens around his neck, it is as if this has unleashed the reality of what is happening. The donkey begins to kick and whine and flail at the men, striking one of them in the leg; I think I hear the fracturing of a bone and it is this that rushes the first taste of bile to my throat.

One of the men strikes the donkey on the side of the head with a gun, buckling his legs, and flopping him to the ground. I can see the shimmer of the sweat, cold-looking sweat, on the flanks of the donkey. The men try pulling him to his feet, and when they push and shove the donkey from behind they can't get a solid grip on his sweaty leather. Then, one of the men stops pushing.

The night holds its breath. Even the luminous voice of the moon has abandoned us.

The man yells something, I don't know what, and he displays his hands and the glow of the moon shows the smeared black paint of the donkey on his palms.

The silence screams. The parrots have stopped for a moment.

The men give up trying to raise the donkey to his feet. A gun is aimed at his head, but the other man places his hand on the rifle.

"No, not the zebra," he says. "My children love the zebra."

The men look at each other. A sorrowful, short bray moans throughout the zoo, throughout all the Gaza Strip, even into and through the tunnels that brought us all here, all except for the donkey, who is a native.

The men leave the pen and the donkey's bray is replaced by the parrots hideous, repetitive thanking of the gunmen as they haul them away in their cage.

※

Now that the secret of the zebra has been revealed, there is heavy mistrust amongst the animals. We sleep with one eye open, seeing only half our nightmares, and those that we do see are unclear. With the parrots now gone, and word that one of the lions has been taken as well, the crowds have become smaller, so small in fact that we are left lulling around for long stretches of time. All of this and it is also December. The days are cooler and the night's cold. I am thankful for my coat of wool, despite its color, and wonder how my friend the gazelle keeps his tiny body warm.

On this night, more than two weeks after the masked men came into the zoo, I visit the gazelle.

"Are you warm enough at night?"

"It isn't too bad yet. Besides, it also gets very cold at night where I come from, out on the veld. You should know that, being from near the desert."

"Yes, but I have this nice coat to keep me warm."

"I may look tiny and frail, but I adapt to all kinds of weather. Besides, I eat a lot more than you think."

"Well, if you ever get cold, you can come and sleep over by the tree. It will help to protect you from the wind."

"Thank you."

There is a quiet between us, not uncomfortably so, but still I am glad the gazelle speaks up.

"How long ago did you know the donkey was no longer a donkey?"

"About a month."

"That's what happened to your face?"

"Yes, but I made a promise not to tell."

"That's nice of you. I too have recently made a promise to someone, but I think I must break it."

I look away.

"Do you want to hear it?"

"I don't know. Isn't hearing something someone promises not to tell almost the same as the one breaking the promise?"

"Possibly, but this promise must be told, I think."

"It's that serious?"

"Yes."

"Tell me then."

"I will not tell you who told me, but it is from someone I trust. A few days ago I heard that Gaza is about to be invaded."

"When are they supposed to invade?"

"Any day, I heard. Maybe even a ground invasion."

"What is going to be done with us?"

"Who knows?"

"Do you think we can escape from here?"

"And where do we go, into the sea?"

"Back through the tunnels."

"You think they will just allow us to leave? Wouldn't that be a strange sight, the two of us, a gazelle and a red sheep roaming the streets of Gaza?"

"What else are we to do?"

"Wait and see what happens. Maybe when the time comes, I will outrun them all." The gazelle smiles his soft smile.

"Lucky for you. I don't think I could outrun much of anything."

"You would be surprised what fear can do for an animal."

Along with the threat of the imminent invasion and the recent attack by the masked gunmen, a paralyzing pallor suffocates the zoo. Word that the gunmen were from Gaza, and that they sold the parrots and lion, leaves us trusting no one. The only time that there is any energy in this place is when the gates open and the customers, although much fewer than before, arrive. There are rumors that the tunnels have been fired upon and are being destroyed. Certainly, we have more and more fighter planes stalking the skies. Without the parrots, the quiet mocks the zoo.

Our food rations have been cut noticeably and it has been nearly a week since they have washed us. Several times the gazelle has taken me up on my offer of him sleeping under the tree—with less food his tiny frame, having lost its natural insulation, becomes colder. Although I have said nothing, there is an odor, not yet entirely unpleasant, on him. I am certain that I too have an ever-growing odor about me, but there is no reason to remind one, particularly a friend, of what he already knows.

Tonight, however, I feel the coursing of a little energy, both in myself and in the zoo, for we have been told that tomorrow several groups of school children will be visiting us. Never have I imagined it would be the case, but I do look forward to the children's candy-sticky fingers through my wool, the cry of their voices, even the agitating tickle of their hands near my ears has a slight appeal to it. And now, without the parrots, and the zebra back to being a donkey, I will, once again, be more of an attraction.

⟋

I sleep very little on this night. It is not the anticipation of the children coming to the zoo that makes me restless, rather it is the scouring of fighter jets, fiery tails spitting out their ass-ends, and the bombs they launch, although striking other parts of the Gaza Strip, still clatter the cages in the zoo. I remain under the tree and cover my eyes with my front hooves, but this does little to help, in fact, it just makes it more uncomfortable for me. I would like to hurry over to the gazelle, but I feel safer under the cover of the tree.

Not until very late in the night does the bombing stop and I drift into an eddying sleep. Soon, that is also shattered when the call to dawn prayers splinters the calm, but this is not the normal call to prayers from atop the minaret, one that rarely awakens me, but rather a warning. The voice of the muezzin shouts to the city that the soldiers and tanks have amassed at the border.

I scurry over to the gazelle, nodding to the donkey, who has not been the same in the head since being struck that night. The gazelle doesn't see me, as he is busy digging a ditch.

"Some night," he says, without turning around.

"Yes," I am surprised that he knows I am behind him.

"What are you digging?"

He stops and comes over to me. I give myself a good shaking and the gazelle begins to pick through my wool, removing, with his mouth, as best he can, the leaves or twigs that have become matted in there during the night. I envy his thin, shiny coat and how easy it is to keep clean. He pauses and sniffs the air.

"Do you smell that?"

"I can smell smoke in the distance."

"Yes, and it has a chemical odor to it."

The gazelle heads over toward the gate and I trail. He turns and walks back to where we just were and back again to the gate; each time we shorten the trip until we are pacing, almost walking in tight circles.

We stop at the gate and look across the way and see the peacock with its beak poking through the bars—a face of gloom. His colorful feathers are closed, making him an ordinary creature. Off to the right, the monkeys squat quietly on rocks. One hangs by his tail from a tree limb.

"Even the consummate entertainers are subdued today," says the donkey, who has been moved back to the petting zoo with us.

The three of us return to the ditch the gazelle was making.

"It feels like those cold, foggy mornings here in Gaza when the cages and fences seem much closer to us than normal. When the cages are cold and you can feel the coldness even without touching it."

We look, collectively, to the brightening sky as though it holds in it the answers to the day ahead. And maybe it does: high clouds have etched their designs above us and there are some lower clouds as well, but these are darker and swell like soft scabs, and it is these, the man-made clouds, which scream much more of the days ahead than those that nature has given to us.

⟋

And the children do not come to visit on this morning. Or on the next. As I, the donkey and the gazelle lie down for the night, in the ditches we have dug, waiting for another night of bombings, I can't imagine there will be any children visiting us tomorrow or on the many tomorrows that number the calendars.

"What's that noise?" I ask of the clanking that grows closer.

"Tanks; the ground invasion must have begun. Stay in the ditch."

I do as the gazelle says, but my curiosity keeps my eyes just above the lip of the ditch. I notice that the gazelle, and the donkey, are peeking as well. And before I see the tank, I hear and feel its crunching feet crumbling through the pathways of the zoo. I see the fence to our pen trampled beneath the tank, like a biscuit in the mouth of a camel. The tank stops, pirouettes, and fires into the cage housing the birds. Peacocks. Doves. Herons. Pigeons. Ostriches. None of us breathe in the ditches. We wait for a call from the birds, but the only sound is the passing of the tanks and the skulking boots of the soldiers.

"Do you think they will come in here?"

"I hope not. Besides, what would they want with the three of us?"

"What did they want with a cage full of dead birds?" I ask.

"Maybe nothing more than to show that they could do it."

In the glow of the burning fires I see coming toward us a lion and he runs full sprint then a single shot castrates the night and the lion crumbles hard, a throaty grunt or growl pierces the zoo and it is over. My eyes tear and I cannot be sure if the gazelle and donkey are also crying or if it is just my eyes that make it appear as such. My nose begins to run profusely and my throat is scoured with heat. The gazelle crawls into my ditch and tells me to cover my face with his body and he does the same against me.

"Tear gas," he squeals.

My face is buried deep into his bony flanks and his in mine and we don't move and I wonder whether we will be next for the animal-thirsty soldiers. A quiet has detained the zoo. Perhaps the soldiers have moved along. Still I keep my face buried into the belly of the gazelle.

Night is the time for bombing and it begins again. Immediately I can tell that it is closer than on the previous nights. One bomb strikes so close that we are lifted from the ditches. When I peek, I see a fire has erupted just beyond our pen and in its glower I see that the tree, under which I have spent nearly every night of the past seven months, has lost its leaves. The first time I was shorn, the nakedness I felt, comes to mind, and this, I think, is what the tree must now feel. I look to the gazelle and he is looking at me. From the corner of my eye a glimmer, whiter even than the beautiful underbelly of my friend, illuminates the sky. Thinking it is only from the fire, I try to ignore it, but its brightness harasses me. I turn toward the magnificent light and watch it drift toward us.

Those summer nights, back in the Sinai, I think. How a group of us sheep, if the gate was left open by mistake, would sneak into the grazing field and watch the dashing of the stars across the coal-black cheeks of the sky. They seemed so close, until tonight that is, when these late December stars parachute out of the sky, so slowly, as if they are taking their time, moseying, in order for us to savor their beauty. Near us, they drop. Their glow softens as they nestle on the ground; some have become like leaves in the tree. Before tonight, I used to imagine stars being cold, but now I see that they still hold the heat from their long, long journeys. Silently they continue to drop, silhouetting a minaret to the east, the monkey cages, the long-necked giraffe that is still leaning against the fence.

Without warning, the donkey leaps out of the ditch.

"Something is burning me!" he yells as he runs.

I chase after the donkey, which is in a panic and darting in circles before falling to the ground and rubbing his side in the dirt.

"What is it?"

"Something is burning me."

"Turn over and let me see."

When he does, the donkey again begins to squeal and rolls back onto his side and rubs viciously into the ground.

"Let me have a look. Just quickly."

When he turns over and exposes his injured side, I see immediately a glow, much like the stars we watched fall only minutes ago, around which oozes greenish pus.

"It is one of the stars that is burning you. Let me try and remove it."

I put my mouth close to the wound, all the while the donkey squirms.

"Hold still. I can't get at it with you moving."

"I'm trying, but it is burning me."

I bite at the small glowing ember and leap back as it brands my tongue. I poke at it with my hoof, but it doesn't come out, as though it is embedded in there. I try to pinch it between my two front hooves and that doesn't help.

"I can't get at it," I say, my mouth already forming a blister. "Let's go back to the ditch before the soldiers see us."

We hurry along; in the ditch, the gazelle is wheezing from the tear gas.

"It is eating away my insides," the gazelle whispers.

The bombing has let up and I haven't seen or heard the soldiers or the tanks for some time now. Fires still flicker, but the stars no longer fall. The donkey is curled in upon himself, as if trying to smother the buried star.

"I'll go for help."

The gazelle turns his head, but doesn't open his eyes.

"Be careful, the soldiers are still out there."

"I will be back soon."

I reach out my hoof and am about to touch the donkey, but stop, afraid that I will cause him more pain. My left hoof remains poised above him for a moment before I place it on the ground and it leads me out of the ditch. I head toward the flattened gate, trying not to look at the dead lion. My throat and lungs still burn. I need a long drink of water.

Outside the pen, not paying attention, I slip on a cluster of feathers. One of them, a peacock feather, is stuck to the bottom of my hoof. I try to shake it off, but it won't come loose. I go to the wall and scrape against it until the feather has fallen. I come to the monkey cage, hoping that their human-like hands can help me with the donkey, but it is quiet; only a crackling fire from a work shed utters a sound. I see nothing inside.

"Are you okay?"

Nothing. I look down; what I at first think is a branch turns out to be a tail of a monkey. Back against a rock I see two monkeys embracing each other in a death hug; one has his mouth open in a hideous final scream. From somewhere in the zoo comes a shrill, almost like that of the peacocks during mating season, but, no, that is not possible. Once more, the shrill. I don't know what to do.

⌒

I must get the gazelle and donkey out of here. I see the giraffe's gangly legs splayed, that long, rubbery tongue hanging lifelessly from his mouth. I stare at this miracle of the Gaza Zoo, somehow brought in through those same tunnels through which I barely fit.

Not paying attention, I nearly step in the bird feathers again. I begin to trot, and as I round the corner, my pen comes into sight and I see a small fire in the distance. I step over the broken gate and head toward the ditch. As I get closer, the fire is a little larger. Faster I move and before I arrive at the ditch, I know what the fire is that chants softly in the night.

―

Above the donkey I stand. His body burns, not angry flames, but blue-green fingers, which are respectful, almost. I begin to kick dirt atop the donkey, to smother the flames as much as to bury him. The gazelle crawls out of the ditch and weakly helps me. I listen, but there is nothing to hear. Could it be that we are the last living animals in the zoo? When finished, I pause, not in prayer, for what good is prayer in all this madness? And even if I did believe in something beyond this place, way out there, somewhere deep in that black void from where those stars dropped, would I want to go to such a place, where such vengeful stars litter the earth with their poison?

I step away from the donkey and a flame pokes out of the ground. A little more dirt I shovel atop it, but another finger is born. And another. Another, until a tiny sacristy has appeared. I turn to my friend and we take one last look at the pen and we walk away, along the paths, past the animals in this zoo, all, like the both of us, from a distant land, caged within the cage of Gaza itself.

―

On the tank-crumbled paths we continue, where, not that many days ago, children ran and stopped and laughed and forgot, for a little while, their lives; adults did so as well, I imagine. We pass silent cages. As we near the entrance, we stop. The both of us need a rest; our lungs have been weakened by the tear gas. I lean against a cage and wait until the tightness in my lungs and throat subsides.

"Are you okay to move on?"

The gazelle nods, but doesn't speak.

We take only a couple of steps before a voice halts us.

"Hey, sheep."

I turn to the voice. There is a broken birdcage on the ground, and not until I hear the voice again do I see the dirty pigeon in the back corner of it.

"Can you help me?"

The cage is ajar and I wonder why the bird doesn't let himself out.

"The door is open."

"My wing, this one here." He motions with his beak to his right wing. "It was injured when the cage fell."

I look at the pigeon's feet, which, unlike many of the pigeons I have seen in my years, are in good condition.

"Why don't you just walk out of the cage?"

"What's a bird that cannot fly? Especially me, for I am no ordinary pigeon. I come from a long lineage of carrier pigeons."

Everyone has a story, I think. I go to the cage and lay flat on my belly. The pigeon stares at me.

"Are you going to get on or not?"

The pigeon leaves the cage and hops onto my back. I stand and go in the direction of the entrance and, leaning against the gate, there is a man. Closer, I see it is the warden, one of the men who tied my legs together and placed me in the zoo, all those many months ago. Farid, his name, the one who also painted me.

Puddled beneath him, a sticky mess of blood. When he hears me, he looks up and chuckles, bringing a grimace to his face. Toward the open gate I look, then back at him. With great pain he tilts his head toward the gate and says: "Go on, little sheep. You are free; I am the warden of the free."

I thank Farid, but I doubt he understands me. Turning toward the gate I see the gazelle twenty yards ahead and running. I want to shout for him to wait, but don't, thinking that I will catch up to him later. Against my neck I feel a pecking and I twist my head and look at the pigeon and he fidgets and pokes at his back.

"What's wrong with you?"

He doesn't answer, but then lets out a long, mournful high-pitched coo. At first, although I know it isn't true, I think it is one of the many wailing ambulances. I turn to the pigeon and see a small flame licking at his back. Surprising me, he begins to flap his wings, even the one he says is injured. Then he is airborne and both wings are afire now and the more he flaps, the more he fans the flames. I watch, mesmerized, as the pigeon climbs as high as the telephone pole, then, the only thing left in the sky is a puff of smoke where, seconds before, the pigeon was. I gaze at the cloud of smoke, as though I have just watched the performance of a sadistic magician, and I wonder if the pigeon was ever on my back at all.

Through the broken gate I look out into the city. Nowhere do I see the gazelle. You are alone, I think, and I step through the threshold of the entrance, now an exit.

Border Shearing (Epilogue)

For now, the missiles have stopped. Hassan and I step into the dark, the dark of war, the dark of childhood nightmares. Off in the distance, over by the sea, billows of smoke have been spewing into the sky after the bombing of the sewage treatment plant forty-eight hours ago. Our excrement pours unabated into the water—our sea, their sea; it doesn't matter. The waves bow and crash as they have always done, but now the tide races upon the shore, recedes, filling its soul with our filth.

Hassan and I leave the clinic where we have taken shelter. We walk past the silhouetted cages; enough of the city is burning to give us some light. The first cage we pass is that of the monkeys; Hassan takes the keys from his belt and opens the lock. We step inside a mass grave. Together we pass birds, a horse, a camel, the only zebra in Gaza. On and on, the litany continues. After coming upon the petting zoo, Hassan puts his arm on my shoulder.

"We need to somehow dispose of them."

I look at him as though he is an idiot. I say nothing.

"Shafiq?"

"Yes. Of course, that is what we must do."

Now, more than any time in my life, what I need is to be alone. The darkness no longer frightens me, nor does the animal graveyard.

"Go and get the wheelbarrow and you can begin at the west end and I will gather the animals at the east end. Bring them to the front of the clinic."

"What will we do with them?"

"We'll have to burn them. There is no other way."

We hurry back toward the clinic. Hassan stops and gets the wheelbarrow from the shed and returns to where we have just come from. I enter the monkey cage. I don't know where to begin. So much joy they brought the children, no, all of us here in Gaza. There was always laughter around this part of the zoo. That is why we placed the monkeys near the front, where people could enter with laughter and take a little of it back with them, whether to the city or Jabaliya or all the way to Khan Yunis, embrace that joy for an hour or a day or allow it to nestle into their nighttime dreams.

I go around to the back of the cage and slide to the ground behind the rocks where the monkeys chased one another, caught the peanuts tossed to them, performed their magic on the people. I bury my face into my filthy jacket and tears choke me and they won't come all the way out, they are just trapped there gathering until they are like a hundred little hands all trying to strangle me; I don't attempt to fight them off. I welcome them, in fact. And it is like this for I don't know how long. Any love that I have is also trapped between my head and heart, coagulating into a sticky lump along with hope and hatred and sadness and love. I can neither swallow nor throw them up. But then, and I don't know how it happens, a scream from somewhere inside me erupts—a forty-year scream—and it is long and mournful and goes on and on until everything is out and the only feeling that is a part of me is numbness, if that is a feeling at all.

_⸝_

I am the anti-Noah. My ark—this zoo—is a death ship.

Hassan and I are at the back end of the zoo, the petting area, gathering the last of the animals. We have just lifted one of the sheep into the wheelbarrow, doing so with great care so that we do not get burned. Embedded in several of the animals, we have found flakes of phosphorus in their wool and fur. A soft bleat comes from the far end of the petting zoo. The both of us turn at the same time; the sound of life has frozen us. We leave behind the wheelbarrow and follow the bleating. Sidled against a tree, a small goat, perhaps two months old.

"Take the wheelbarrow back and I will follow you with the goat."

With care I lift the goat and cradle him in my arms, but he begins to flail in pain. I place him back on the ground and look for where he is hurt. I find the lower parts of both rear legs to be injured, along with numerous shrapnel wounds.

"I know this is going to hurt, my little friend, but only for a second until I get you on my back," I whisper into its twitching ear.

The bleats are high-pitched, but once I have secured the goat onto my back, it begins to calm down. I walk with care, but as quickly as I can. Impossible not to think of my grandfather, Ghassan, six decades ago.

I place the goat on the operating table and pull the light cord, but, of course, there is no light. I know this, but still pull the cord twice more.

"Shafiq."

I look up and see Hassan framed in the doorframe.

"There is no light," I say to him. "The goat is not strong enough. Without removing the shrapnel, he will certainly die."

Hassan studies the room and then the goat.

"Perhaps there is a way," he says, rushing out of the building.

I remain behind, trying to calm the shivering goat. I turn to the sound of the screeching wheel of the wheelbarrow. Hassan pushes it into the clinic. One of the dead sheep is inside. Coming from the wool, a soft tongue of flame.

"What are you doing?"

"I think the sheep can provide us with enough light to operate on the goat. But we must be fast."

"We can't do this."

"We must, Shafiq. What better homage to life than for the dead to extend the life of another?"

Hassan settles the wheelbarrow next to the operating table. A cone of light rises from the sheep. Hassan goes to the corner and hauls over a large mirror, bracing it against the wall opposite the wheelbarrow. Now, twin tongues toggle the room. I grab the pliers and begin to remove the larger pieces of the shrapnel. Clink, clink, they drop onto the metal table. Hassan holds the goat. The fire from the sheep grows and with it so too does the smell of garlic, the telltale sign of white phosphorus.

I feel through the goat's fur, locating the shrapnel and then removing it. I reach for the bottle of rubbing alcohol and drop it onto the floor. I look down at it, not bending to pick it up, but brace my hands against the table. I begin to shake and the shaking leads to sobbing and the sobbing to Hassan grabbing me by the left arm while steadying the goat with his right.

"What is it, Shafiq?"

"I can't go on."

"But you're almost done and the goat will live."

"No, Hassan. This place; I can't go on in this place. It's killing me, if I am not already dead. There is nothing left of me. When I look into a mirror, I see a dead man."

"It's a bad time, Shafiq. Only a bad time and it will pass."

"And then what? What happens when this bad time passes?"

Hassan looks into the mirror and the fire of the slowly burning sheep wriggles in its reflection.

"I need to escape the prison of my sorrow, Hassan."

Staring into the growing flame, I hear, not the goat with life, but the sheep in its death. I try hard, but cannot make out what it is saying. The greenish flame pecks at our faces in the mirror, mesmerizing me. A peacefulness hovers over the room. Nothing moves. The slightest of breaths cannot be heard. For a minute, I almost feel alive, but then a burst of light, and the fire erupts, devouring the both of us in the mirror.

⌐

Two soldiers smash into the clinic. They look at the burning sheep and then at me and the goat. When their guns are aimed at us, both Hassan and I raise our hands high. The goat scrabbles on the metal table and finds enough footing to leap onto the floor and dart between the soldier's legs and out the door. One of the soldiers turns and runs out, takes aim and fires.

"Run, my little friend!" I shout. "Run!"

The frantic clopping of the tiny hooves become distant until no more. A smile finds its way to my face.

We are led at gunpoint out of the clinic and down the northern street of the zoo.

The garlic-like odor remains clotted in my nostrils. I want to ask Hassan if he also smells it or is it my imagination. I have enough sense not to talk. We pass several of the coffin-like cages. I cannot bring myself to look into them again.

"Stop there."

My arms are still raised and I do not turn around to face the voice.

"Toss us the keys."

I do as the soldier demands.

"You, too."

Hassan does the same.

The soldier points his rifle first at the both of us and then to the cage which once housed the lion. Again, a poke of the rifle toward the cage. We go inside. I think I will never live to have a child; think that now that the zoo has been destroyed I have left nothing of myself in this world; wish that they would take and shoot us on the beach, where, once more I could see the fold of the waves. The slamming of the cage door startles me, thinking it is gunshots.

"This is where you belong."

The sound of the boots fades. The both of us remain silent and where we stand. Hassan is the first to move and he goes over to the door and rattles it, but it is locked. He points to the back wall of the cage. Painted on the wall, in the language of the soldiers, two simple words, a syllable each. *You Lost.* I manage to move my legs the five steps to the rocks and large tree stump. I remember the day that we hauled all of this inside the lion cage. There was so much excitement—true joy—that in a week's time the first lion in Gaza would arrive. And it did and was the most popular of all the animals in the zoo. Even more than the monkeys. Some days I would just stand outside the cage and watch the eyes of both the children and adults. This is what I intended when a group of us came up with the idea for the zoo six years ago. Ironic, I had always thought, how we find so much joy in seeing the animals in their cages. I close my eyes fantasizing of the rebirth of our once-fierce lion, a lion that once again had all its teeth and claws and heroism and it jumped out from behind the rocks, past Hassan and I, and, with a few vicious swats with its paws, he strikes the soldiers one by one by one.

But now, of course, the irony only grows; the zookeeper, the anti-Noah, locked inside a cage. I hear a distant baaaah of a sheep.

"Shut up."

"What?" Hassan asks.

"Sorry. I didn't mean to speak aloud. I was only telling the sheep to shut up."

Again, another baaaah.

A single gunshot blisters the Gaza night.

It is May, late into a Gaza night. During the day, any signs of spring have been strangled by the heat, but now, at this hour, with the wooden shutters open, the American can savor the caress of the cool sea air. Usually on nights such as this, when the wind comes in from the west, the American can hear the distant chant of the sea.

But on this night, as on so many nights, it is the sound of the footsteps of Bassam that he hears; at first, when he wakes, he thinks it is part of his dream, but then remembers that his friend is spending the night in the small apartment the American stays in when traveling to the more distant camps in the south.

He thought Bassam would like to stay a night or two away from Jabaliya, but he has been anxious the entire day, and now, his pacing brings the American out of his bedroom.

Bassam is in the kitchen making Turkish coffee.

"Couldn't sleep?"

"I am not used to being away from the camp. You want some coffee?"

"A little. When was the last time you spent a night away from Jabaliya?"

"Other than when I was in prison, never."

The American watches Bassam lift the coffee pot from the stove after its first boil. When the coffee settles, he places it back above the fire until the foam rises a second time. Bassam turns off the stove and sets the pot on the counter.

"Why don't you stay in Jabaliya?"

"You mean extend my stay?"

"No, stay."

While Bassam is pouring the coffee, the American rests his hand on his friend's shoulder.

"After visiting my family, I am going to Sudan."

"Why Sudan?"

"Do you remember when we were playing backgammon and the boy with the bird approached us?"

"Of course, but what does that have to do with you not staying?"

"I can't really explain all this, but it was that night that I knew for certain that telling your people's story, and others like it, that there is no greater way to live my life."

"Ironic, isn't it? How so many people who are free are trying to escape home, while others, who can't go back, are dying to return."

―

On his final night in Jabaliya, the American goes to watch a soccer match between two teams from the camp. The players do not wear uniforms; one team plays with shirts on, the other shirtless. The match is physical, tackles are aggressive, harsh words are shouted back and forth. Shafiq and the American sit on the side of a hill, saying little. At the end of the match, a fight breaks out between several players and soon spreads to others. The American asks what they are fighting about.

"A couple of the players on the other team are accused of being collaborators with the army. Come on, we need to hurry home ."

There is almost nothing said on the way to block number four. The American and Shafiq hug.

"I will see you later tonight at the farewell party."

Again, they hug. Shafiq walks into the alley heading into block number five. The American waits for him to turn around. First, Shafiq's hands and feet fade, then the back of his head. The American continues to watch until Shafiq's white robe also disappears, leaving nothing but darkness.

―

In these the final hours of his months in Jabaliya, the grandmother, Fatima, hands him a metal tub, saying that she cannot send him back across the continent, across the ocean, and to his mother, without being clean. He takes the large metal tub, places it on the rutted cement floor of the shower and stands under the trickle of lukewarm water.

While taking his shower, he thinks of what his friend, Shafiq, has told him, just a few days before: that when he returns to his country, his family *and friends would no longer recognize him. This will be the indelible scar that Jabaliya will leave behind.*

Drying himself with the threadbare towel, less than five hours before the taxi will pick him up and take him to the airport, he realizes the truth of those words.

Although he promised that he would stop and say goodbye, Shafiq does not come to the farewell dinner. Instead, he climbs a ladder onto the roof of one of the houses and watches the American standing on School Street, alone, in the final minutes before the call to prayer, the last minutes of his final curfew.

He watches the American's silhouette emerge and the silhouettes of those walking up and down School Street to say their goodbyes. There are handshakes and hugs, even the grandmother, Fatima, embraces him, and tears are coming from the tough young boys who, in a few hours, on their way to school and back, will fight the gun-toting soldiers with stones and Molotov cocktails.

The taxi arrives, trailed by the thigh-high dust of mid-summer. He throws his backpack into the trunk and there are final embraces before the taxi pulls away. Staring out the back window, he looks down the street and then up at the roof that his friend is on. Shafiq gives him a sad wave of the hand, but cannot tell if the American returns the wave, leaving him, for the remainder of his life, wondering whether he has been seen or, perhaps, has been mistaken for a large piece of firewood or a water tank or even a talking goat.

As Far As One Can Go

With the engine idling, and his long-time driver smoking inside the car, the last veterinarian in Jabaliya rests his foot on the back bumper, studying dawn in the only place he has ever known. He thinks of his wife inside the house, certain that she is doing the same, trying to sear into her eyes the smallest of details, those we see all our lives, but never seem to remember.

Forty minutes remain before the call to prayers will rattle the Gaza Strip, by which time the veterinarian hopes to be through the city and heading south. He knows that the longer they wait the more difficult this day will be; still, surprising himself, he tempers the urge to hurry his wife. The veterinarian is quite comfortable here with the feel of the bumper against his foot and the morning calm and the slow vanquishing of the stars. Besides, he cannot yell out for his wife to hurry for he would risk waking someone and this day must be kept a secret. In fact, it was only two nights ago that he told his wife the news. As he went to kiss her good night he whispered it, as one would whisper words of passion to a lover, words that you wanted no one else to hear. She showed no real emotion at first; it was something that they had talked about in the past, although briefly, but then suddenly she had started to cry and he held her tightly, as much to muffle her tears as to comfort her.

And it was only last night, six or seven hours ago, that he texted his long-time driver, Hassan, telling him that he needed to go somewhere very early the next morning. From the corner of his eye the veterinarian catches the comet-like glow of the driver's cigarette, which he has flung out the window of the car. He watches until it disappears.

How things come full circle, he thinks.

It was in this exact place, nearly four decades ago, as a young boy, that the veterinarian stood in the bathroom and saw, through the window, six feet above his head, a trail of red racing by and then vanishing. Two seconds at most. At first, he thought it was a flare shot by the army. He said nothing that night, but several more times that week it happened again, nearly at the same time, just before eight o'clock. The boy dismissed the idea that it was a flare and he thought, hoped was more accurate, that it was a red star cutting across the sky. On the sixth night, he waited for his grandfather to come inside and the boy told him what he had seen. His grandfather gave the boy a sad-eyed smile and said nothing to him of how, each night, he flipped a finished cigarette into the air and it was this that the boy saw. Then, the boy's grandfather bolted the door and shuttered the windows, including the bathroom, hoping to confine curfew out in the streets.

⚊

The driver stares at the cigarette somersaulting through the air until the sparks cough against the street and slowly suffocate. The early hour is not a surprise, for he has been called many times, and with much less notice, but the fact that the vet's wife will be coming along—that is unusual. He can recall a handful of times, in all these years, that the both of them were together in the car.

When the vet removes his foot from the bumper, the driver waits for the door to open. Only once did he ever get out of the car and open the door for him. It was that first day, more than a decade ago, and the vet said nothing to the driver, holding open the back door of the white, early-model Peugeot until they were both inside, and in the rear view mirror their eyes met and the vet spoke these simple words:

"Only when I am too old to open the door myself, only then should you do so for me."

Now he waits and wonders where he will be taking the two of them, for there are not all that many possibilities, at this time of day, or anytime really, here in the Gaza Strip.

⚊

The day she woke with morning sickness, twelve weeks before, Ahlam noticed for the first time the hairline crack in the bottom of her favorite pan. She studies it now and is tempted to take it with her, but her husband warned her to leave everything in the house untouched—*carry them only in the suitcase of memories* were his exact words. She imagines cooking in another pan, the weight of it, the feel of its handle in her grip as she coaxes the eggs or potatoes or beans. More to the touch, than sight, the crack can be seen.

She flattens her palm against the pan and keeps it there until the soft squeal of the car door nudges her from the kitchen. She stops and inhales a deep pull of the house, holds it in her lungs for as long as possible, then turns back to the kitchen and grabs her favorite wooden spoon, her grandmother's wooden spoon, and tucks it inside her dress, next to the large metal key from their house, a house she has only heard stories of, where this same grandmother was born all those years before.

―

They are halfway through the camp before the veterinarian tells the driver to take the coastal road and another few minutes will pass before he speaks again.

"Do you know the temperature of the sea this time of year, Hassan?"

The driver glances at the veterinarian, staring out at the black sea, hems of white the only thing that tells you it is there, that and the knowledge that it has always been there.

"I'm not sure. Sometimes, as a child, I would go with my family and we would swim there. I don't ever remember it being all that cold. That was in summer though, not the end of September."

"I have never been in the sea. I have walked along the beach, of course, but never swum in it."

"We used to go north of Beach Camp and play there, but it was dangerous because of the remains of an old port at the bottom. My Uncle told us that many children hit their heads on the jagged walls while diving."

The call to prayers starts up in the distance and they listen. The chisel of the morning sun chips away the sea's black sheet revealing a giant slab of slate. The driver asks the veterinarian if he would like to stop at one of the mosques in the city.

"No, Hassan. Let's keep going. Wait, stop the car. Stop the car!"

The driver pulls to the side of the road.

"What is it?"

The veterinarian is already out of the car, leaving the door open, and he turns to the driver.

"I just saw the gazelle in that alleyway over there," he says, pointing to the cluster of buildings on the street opposite the sea.

"Gazelle?"

The veterinarian runs in front of the car and into the alleyway and the driver watches the silhouette until it is lost in the puzzle of the side streets.

~

The driver asks the veterinarian's wife if she saw the gazelle.

"There were a couple of goats picking at something along the roadside."

"Maybe that is what he saw. It is still rather dark."

"He has been obsessed with that animal ever since the invasion. He has dreams about it sometimes."

"It was a beautiful animal."

"I remember when they first brought the gazelle to the zoo; Shafiq slept there for a couple of nights. That was the only time in his life he didn't sleep in Jabaliya. Tonight, Allah willing, will be the third."

"Maybe he did see the gazelle," the driver says, noticing in the mirror that she is holding a wooden spoon.

"Don't forget that Shafiq's grandfather believed he once had a goat that could talk."

~

Nearly half an hour has passed and her husband has yet to return. And now the driver has gone out looking for him and she is getting restless and wants to stand outside the car, but doesn't, for she cannot risk being seen. The sun pries through the window, flailing against the back of her head. It has been a couple of weeks since her morning sickness ended, but the sun is curdling her stomach. She rolls down the window, hoping the sea will soothe her, but looking out at the enormity of it, its endless expanse, only adds to her anxiety.

She feels as she did two nights ago, when Shafiq told her of what they were about to do and her mind spun and she tried to gather her emotions, although it was impossible. He reached down and touched her stomach and left his hand there and spoke of the baby and how others had done what they were about to do. Everything, at that moment, began to slow down and somehow seemed all right. But then he started up about not telling anyone, not even their families or best friends. No one. Leave without a word. That is when she started to cry and strike her fists into her husband's back, which he allowed her to do. And she cried. And fell asleep. And she woke with fists clenched and twenty-four hours to strangle an acidic secret.

But now those hours have passed and it is the present and her mother and uncles and nieces and brothers are waking to a day, another day, no different, they believe, than the normal dullness of the unchanging hours of the stultifying tick-tock of Jabaliya. And soon they would be expecting her for lunch and when she doesn't show, someone would go to the house and look in on her and the door will be open, for she left it that way, and everything will be the same as always, except, of course, she would not be there.

The car has become a tomb and she opens the door and walks around to the front driver's seat and sits behind the wheel for the first time in her life. She presses the horn and it screams, startling her, but she doesn't let up, and the longer she presses the more she feels that she will be heard.

The veterinarian reaches the car first, but there are already several vehicles pulled off the roadside, checking on the chaos. Some of the people are out of the cars and standing there yelling for the woman to stop blaring the horn.

The veterinarian pushes past the crowd.

"Everything is okay. It is my wife. Thank you for stopping to help."

They look at him, and although backing up a few steps, no one leaves. He doesn't recognize any of them and for that he is thankful. He tries the door and it is locked; he goes around the car and the other doors are as well. Tapping on the front window doesn't get her attention. Her head rests against the steering wheel, both hands pressing the horn. He begins pounding on the window, but still the horn drones. In the reflection, he sees that more people have gathered, but he also sees and hears his driver.

"Go on, get out of here. There's nothing of interest to any of you. Get out!"

As before, the onlookers back away, however, most remain.

"What's happening, Shafiq?" he asks in a low voice.

"She has locked herself in the car."

The driver hands Shafiq the keys and approaches the crowd.

"Why don't you all show some respect and leave the man alone?"

The driver stares at them, one by one, until they slip into their cars or get back to their walks along the beach, but then, suddenly, a hush, a loud hush, pummels the morning. Those who have begun driving away, the others that have their feet once again digging into the sand, all turn back in the direction of the quiet and see the woman out of the car in the embrace of her husband and they look and pause and wonder what it was all about. Then they move along, as does the day, and in a short while so too do the driver, the veterinarian, and his wife get back into the car and continue in the direction of south.

⌐

They drive with the city on their left, the sea to their right, and of course the sea will go on forever whereas the city will soon be past them.

"Did you find your gazelle?" she asks with a chill in her voice.

"No, it must have gotten away."

"I didn't know that goats were so elusive."

"I, of all people, don't you think, would know the difference between a goat and a gazelle?"

"Where are we going, Shafiq?" asks the driver.

"South, until we can go no further."

⌐

In the early months of the Gaza Zoo, sometimes two or three times a week, the veterinarian and the driver would make this trip to the border. There they would pick up animals that were brought through the tunnels; smaller animals mostly—birds and lambs and, once, even a monkey. Since these animals usually were not drugged for the harrowing half-mile journey beneath the border, they were often in a panic when in the car. Once, a monkey reached through the cage in the back seat and grabbed a hold of the driver's ear, nearly causing a crash.

"What are you laughing about, Hassan?" the veterinarian asks.

"I was just thinking of our adventure with the monkey."

The veterinarian smiles a soft smile of recall. He removes his glasses and rubs his eyes and plows his hand through his thick, gray-speckled hair.

"This is a difficult place to live."

The driver says nothing as he studies the veterinarian gazing out the window as he speaks.

"I have never seen an animal in the wild, Hassan. Imagine that; me, a veterinarian."

Up ahead, the buildings of the border camp and town of Rafah come into view. The driver begins to slow.

"Please don't slow down, Hassan."

"Sorry, Shafiq."

"The sooner we get there, the better. But, thank you."

"There is no need to explain or to thank me."

"It's so damn difficult to breathe in this place. People should not have to struggle just to breathe, Hassan. I owe my child something better. Even if I die trying."

They pass to the east of the most southerly of the eight refugee camps in Gaza and even though the mid-morning sun is hot and uncomfortable, they keep the windows up for the dust is nearly roof-high.

↗

Everything has been arranged beforehand, and within minutes the three of them are at the mouth of one of the tunnels. First, the veterinarian's wife goes down the fifteen steps of the ladder before yelling that she has made it. The two men hug. The veterinarian is a few steps down the ladder, his head even with the top rung, and he looks up and tells the driver that the car is his and asks him to wait until tomorrow to let his family know where they have gone.

With that the veterinarian goes, rung after rung, into the throat of the tunnel. The driver leans over the hole, trying to get one last look at his friend, but his head blocks the noon-high sun, rendering the hole bottomless.

⌐

The afternoon dissolves with the driver sitting in the car, twenty yards from the tunnel. When night slams the shutters on the day, the driver turns on the low-beams and angles the car so that they cast their light on the white tarp that now covers the entrance.

Struggling to keep awake, the driver finally succumbs to sleep. Soon, there comes a knock on the window. Startled, the driver wakes and he is overwhelmed by a rush of joy and a few seconds pass before he recognizes that it is not Shafiq standing there, but one of the tunnel workers.

The man is saying something, but the driver cannot understand, then he rolls down the window and hears the last of the man's words.

"... made it."

"What's that?"

"They have made it through the tunnel and to Egypt."

⌐

Still he stays the night at the border, turning off the lights of the car, sitting atop the hood, which has retained, for a short while, the warmth from the engine. A man brings him some coffee and they talk.

"Are many people smuggled through the tunnels?"

"Not many. First, you need a contact on the other side, or enough bribe money, or both. And the people have to go through one of the smaller tunnels, which is dangerous and not at all easy."

"Did it really take them all this time to go less than half a mile?"

"You try crawling that far in a tunnel, with panic sucking from you what little air there is. And your friends, their journey has just started."

"Do you know Shafiq?"

"I know of him because of the animals that came through here."

"We are no different than them," the driver says.

The man looks as if he will say something, but the words are clotted in his throat, and he stabs the ground repeatedly with the toe of his shoe, as if the words were somehow entombed there.

~

Literally days after the four decades of occupation ended, second floors began to sprout atop the sixty-year-old cement block houses in Jabaliya, something that was illegal under the military. Everything that cluttered the roofs had to be removed before the new floor was added. No longer are the military watchtowers the highest structures in the camp—they were the first to go. Now there are towers all along the border, two miles away, but from here one cannot see them, unless you are trying to. Walls, still graffiti-stained, now speak in tongues of sparing factions, rather than against the occupation.

Through the remainder of September and well into October, as the driver goes about Jabaliya looking for passengers, he takes in all these things. Why haven't I noticed these changes, he wonders.

Business is slow. During the first weeks he drove up and down and across the streets of Jabaliya, sometimes he sat outside the market, but passengers were a rarity and when he did find one, he often knew them and refused the coin they offered, settling for an apple or a couple of *falafel* as payment. As of late he goes to the city, where business is a little better, but still the days are long and monotonous.

At times, the passengers complain of the odor of animals, something he no longer notices, but is certain it is present. He thinks of the animals that he and the veterinarian brought in the back seat of the car and it wasn't only their behavior that told of their distress, but also the smell of it. Some passengers refuse to ride in his car and they look for another taxi, and with them he doesn't haggle. Sometimes he even opens the back door and thanks them when they get out.

More and more, as of late, the driver leaves the house early in the morning and takes the coastal road and pulls off to the side and walks the streets looking for the elusive gazelle. Other days, he will stand, leaning against the car, gauging the mood of the sea. A sea that acts more like winter, rough and dark and brooding, than an October sea.

~

The driver finds it interesting that whenever he is any way in contact with his car, be it, as he is now, leaning against the hood, or sitting inside it or while driving through Gaza, that he is constantly nagged by thoughts of the lack of business. Each person that passes his car seems to mock him and it becomes too much and he goes inside the shop across the street and orders a coffee and waterpipe. He sits alone in the back corner, enjoying the low light and the pleasant murmur of conversations, and, most of all, the break from the pestering voice inside his head.

On his way out of the shop, the conversation of several fishermen stops him. They are talking of a boat that left Tripoli, hauling refugees. The driver lingers, hoping to hear more, afraid to hear more, but the conversation shifts as the tides do each day and the driver heads to his car, sitting there empty as usual.

↙

To learn of the rumors and the news and the innuendos of the sea, one must go no further than the fishermen who take from it. The driver parks his car in the early morning and walks along the beach, where the fishing boats soak in the sun after their long nights in the water. One morning, he sees one of the fishermen from that afternoon a couple of days before in the teahouse. He recognizes the man by the missing right earlobe. With his toes entwined in the green fishing net, the fisherman speaks without looking up.

"I could feel the death in the sea that morning, could smell it in the nets and taste it in the fish."

The fisherman takes the silence of the driver as disbelief.

"The sea is my mother, my wife, my children. One just knows when there is death in the family."

This time he looks up from the net and the driver turns his head toward the coastal road.

"Do you know someone who may have been taken by the sea?"

"I am not sure."

"But it is possible?"

"Yes. It is very possible."

↙

Most days, he sees the same fisherman and they talk. On a crisp morning that spoke in the voice of the encroaching winter, the driver has to help the fisherman up from the sand.

"Let me give you a ride home."

"No. I am fine once I get moving. It's this damn weather that stiffens my back."

"My car's right there. It's not a problem."

The driver goes to open the door for the fisherman, but hesitates when he is slapped by the memory of the veterinarian. They both stand there, the driver with his hand on the door handle.

"You okay?" asks the fisherman.

"I was just thinking about an old friend of mine."

"Does this happen to be the friend that you are worried about?"

"Yes. I was his driver for many years."

"And was he on the boat from Tripoli?"

"He and his wife may have been. They left Gaza in September."

"Were they trying to go to Italy?"

"I'm not sure, but the morning I drove them to the border, he asked me of the temperature of the sea, which I found strange. Now, I think, that is why he was asking."

The fisherman digs at his fingernails with a hook and asks: "Have you ever seen the desert cry?"

The driver starts the car.

"Is such a thing even possible?"

They sit there and the engine idles and the dark sea bows and crashes and sprints until it can go no further, then it races in retreat and joins the chorus of the water as it has done for so very long, before a single person was even here to witness it.

What the fisherman says is astonishing.

Nearly a year after the *tsunami* slammed Japan, a large Japanese fishing tanker has been found drifting near the west coast of Canada, more than four thousand miles away.

"Did the sea tell you this?" he asks.

"No, our sea only tells of its stories. This is a story from an ocean. I read about it on the Internet."

The driver laughs after hearing this even more astounding news.

"The Internet?"

"Yes, I get stories of the other seas at the internet café on Salah al-Din Street."

Both men laugh and it feels good and neither of them questions it, nor do they dare delve into the bleakness of the last time they have done so.

⟋

Some days the driver goes to the beach later in the morning after his friend, the fisherman, has gone home to sleep. Rarely, but every once in a while, when an unexpected warmth enters him, he will allow himself to imagine, while scouring the beach, that the vet and his wife and now a child are in some old city on the continent across the great sea, and they are watching their child wander and play in the streets made of cobblestone. Or maybe the driver will close his eyes, never walking a step further for fear of missing something important in the flotsam, and he will let his mind roam, seeing the vet working in a small clinic, taking care of the pets—the cats and dogs and hamsters—of the people in a village where the borders are simply crossed. Possibly, the vet works in the one of the zoos, but somehow the driver doubts this.

But these moments, these afternoons of the imagination, are the exception.

Nearly every day, hours before the fishermen begin to congregate along the sand, before they launch their boats into the water, the driver walks the beach, tense like on those distant nights when, as a teen, he used to go out with his friends into the camp and paint anti-occupation slogans on the walls—this is the tension that burdens him when out here walking. He returns home on these days, debilitated, not physically so much as mentally, for his concentration has been so acute.

⟋

At home on this night the driver goes to the back of the house, in the unsettled darkness, and he brings out the ladder that reaches the top of the twelve-foot-high wall. He can't recall the last time he used the ladder, but the memory of the long, jagged scar etched into his brother's back is vivid after all the years. He recalls his brother's feet disappearing through the foot-high gap between the top of the wall and the corrugated roof as the soldiers broke down the front door. Eighteen months later, he saw his brother again, the six-inch scar worming along his back, and he touched it and he remembers it feeling as though something were alive in there.

Now he rests his arms on the wall and his head atop them. He listens to something scuttling across one of the nearby rooftops, a mouse perhaps, more than likely a cat, and nearby there is the hum of a television. A man passes through the alleyway below and the driver wonders whether he can be seen up here. The footsteps of the man fade and someone has turned off the television and there is not much more for his ears.

The wooden ladder creaks as he adjusts his feet. He looks down into the two rooms of his house and they seem different from up here— bigger, yet at the same time, shrunken. Maybe it is the lack of light, but probably it has more to do with the perspective. He will leave the ladder where it is and tomorrow, with the light of the sun, will climb it once again to see the house anew.

A pang of loneliness inundates him, catching him off balance. Still staring at the inside of his barren house, the driver thinks of his brother and how, after being released from prison he left Jabaliya for Kuwait, leaving him with a dying father and no one else. But then he was hired by the vet, giving his days a purpose for the next dozen years and he was able to ignore the mundaneness of his life, the vice-like grip of this place, the contemptuous voices when you come upon the sea or the vengeful land borders north, east and south. *You can go no further*, the words spit into your face.

And it is this, he thinks, these words that drive our young to kill themselves while killing others; this that serves as our shovels to burrow the tunnels; this that brings us to all fours, crawling for hours in the hopes of finding a place where we *can* go further. Isn't this what we all want and need and strive for: to be able to go a little further? And when there is no hope to do so, isn't this when we are at our most vulnerable?

The driver turns his head back to the opening between the roof and the wall. He listens some more to the night sounds in Jabaliya and he thinks he can hear the inhales and exhales of the sea. He doubts that this could be true from such a distance, but forces himself to think otherwise, to believe that this is what he hears.

—

Leaving the ladder against the wall, the driver gets into the car and goes down School Street. As he approaches the giant willow, he shuts off the engine and allows the gravity of the street to take him to the market. He restarts the engine and passes the Martyrs' Cemetery, the newest and largest resting place in Jabaliya. He comes upon the coastal road and drives south, then turns abruptly and stops with the car facing the beach and the sea.

The driver finds a cool place on the steering wheel, a place where his hands haven't warmed it, and he rests his head and it feels good. Taking his foot off the brake, he presses the pedal to the floor and the car lunges onto the beach and over the bumps of the uneven sand. He shuts off the headlights and only the pinpricks of light from the fishing boats—the galaxy of the sea—can be seen. When the car hits the tide-wet sand and the water, it stalls and the driver is thrown against the steering wheel. He sits there calmly and hears a wave crashing and feels it bump against the car and rush past the wheels and then tug the car as it reverses its course.

This is as far as you can go, he thinks.

He opens the door and steps into the cold ankle-high water and is surprised that the sea can hold such a chill. Reaching back into the car, he searches for the flashlight under the seat, finds and switches it on. The dim path of the light guides him and he doubts that the batteries will hold out until sunrise. He takes his time scanning the beach, looking for any hint of the veterinarian and his wife. He comes across several shells, a water bottle, a splinter of wood, the remains of a half-eaten fish.

He continues on until the flashlight flickers and blinks and finally goes blind. He bangs it against his thigh, but it isn't resuscitated. Seeing the ghost of the car down the beach, he thinks of waiting in it until the sun comes up and the fishermen return and they can help him push it out. Although he is cold, the driver walks away from the damp sand to where it is drier and he sits there and looks up at the stars and wonders what they look like from across the sea or over the desert or from anywhere other than here.

Out on the sea the lights of a fishing boat grow larger and this reminds the driver of the Japanese vessel that drifted across the ocean. Nearly a year it took. And as he has done every day since hearing this story, the driver thinks of the veterinarian and his wife and wonders how long it will take for any hint of them to wash upon this ancient shore. How long, he wonders, for a sandal or a suitcase carrying only memories or a key that no longer has a house to unlock?

The American continues to wander, to gather stories: to Egypt and Sudan; Japan and North Korea and China; to many cities in his own country.

Sometimes, when alone on a secluded beach or on a mountain before dawn or in bed at night, he thinks of his bundle of stories, the need to tell them, and how they have become enmeshed with his, to where now there is no longer a border dividing them.

～

But there is this one, a moment he will carry with him to the grave.

He is sitting in the chaos of Gaza City, not far from the place where he first arrived ten weeks before. It is an April day and he wishes it would rain, but knows that he will have left Gaza long before it ever does again. This thought, leaving, both excites and saddens him. It is a rare person in Gaza that can even dream of this. And maybe this is not even possible; can one dream of something that they cannot even fathom? And here he sits, pining about a few months.

He is taking a break from many hours of walking. A soldier on patrol looks at him, he at the soldier, both framed by a fruit vendor's stall. The shutters of shops rattle, unraveling to the ground as merchants close for the afternoon general strike. He has another hour to go to Jabaliya and he tries coaxing himself up off his backpack on which he sits.

Looking up, and through the madness of the city, the American sees a young girl, wearing a white headscarf, walking over to him. Shyly she smiles and hands him a bottle of Gaza 7-UP. He thanks her, holding up his hand for her to wait. Digging into his backpack, he finds a small doll, which he gives to the girl. Many times over the years, he thinks of this moment and knows that the young girl, now a woman, still has with her, the doll, and, he, the story.

～

Books from Etruscan Press

Zarathustra Must Die | Dorian Alexander
The Disappearance of Seth | Kazim Ali
Drift Ice | Jennifer Atkinson
Crow Man | Tom Bailey
Coronology | Claire Bateman
What We Ask of Flesh | Remica L. Bingham
The Greatest Jewish-American Lover in Hungarian History | Michael Blumenthal
No Hurry | Michael Blumenthal
Choir of the Wells | Bruce Bond
Cinder | Bruce Bond
The Other Sky | Bruce Bond and Aron Wiesenfeld
Peal | Bruce Bond
Poems and Their Making: A Conversation | Moderated by Philip Brady
Crave: Sojourn of a Hungry Soul | Laurie Jean Cannady
Toucans in the Arctic | Scott Coffel
Body of a Dancer | Renée E. D'Aoust
Scything Grace | Sean Thomas Dougherty
Areas of Fog | Will Dowd
Surrendering Oz | Bonnie Friedman
Nahoonkara | Peter Grandbois
The Candle: Poems of Our 20th Century Holocausts | William Heyen
The Confessions of Doc Williams & Other Poems | William Heyen
The Football Corporations | William Heyen
A Poetics of Hiroshima | William Heyen
Shoah Train | William Heyen
September 11, 2001: American Writers Respond | Edited by William Heyen
American Anger: An Evidentiary | H. L. Hix
As Easy As Lying | H. L. Hix
As Much As, If Not More Than | H. L. Hix
Chromatic | H. L. Hix
First Fire, Then Birds | H. L. Hix
God Bless | H. L. Hix
I'm Here to Learn to Dream in Your Language | H. L. Hix
Incident Light | H. L. Hix
Legible Heavens | H. L. Hix

Lines of Inquiry | H. L. Hix
Rain Inscription | H. L. Hix
Shadows of Houses | H. L. Hix
Wild and Whirling Words: A Poetic Conversation | Moderated by H. L. Hix
All The Difference | Patricia Horvath
Art Into Life | Frederick R. Karl
Free Concert: New and Selected Poems | Milton Kessler
Who's Afraid of Helen of Troy: An Essay on Love | David Lazar
Parallel Lives | Michael Lind
The Burning House | Paul Lisicky
Quick Kills | Lynn Lurie
Synergos | Roberto Manzano
The Gambler's Nephew | Jack Matthews
The Subtle Bodies | James McCorkle
An Archaeology of Yearning | Bruce Mills
Arcadia Road: A Trilogy | Thorpe Moeckel
Venison | Thorpe Moeckel
So Late, So Soon | Carol Moldaw
The Widening | Carol Moldaw
Cannot Stay: Essays on Travel | Kevin Oderman
White Vespa | Kevin Oderman
Mr. Either/Or | Aaron Poochigian
The Dog Looks Happy Upside Down | Meg Pokrass
The Shyster's Daughter | Paula Priamos
Help Wanted: Female | Sara Pritchard
American Amnesiac | Diane Raptosh
Human Directional | Diane Raptosh
Saint Joe's Passion | JD Schraffenberger
Lies Will Take You Somewhere | Sheila Schwartz
Fast Animal | Tim Seibles
One Turn Around the Sun | Tim Seibles
A Heaven Wrought of Iron: Poems From the Odyssey | D. M. Spitzer
American Fugue | Alexis Stamatis
The Casanova Chronicles | Myrna Stone
Luz Bones | Myrna Stone
The White Horse: A Colombian Journey | Diane Thiel
The Arsonist's Song Has Nothing to Do With Fire | Allison Titus
The Fugitive Self | John Wheatcroft
YOU. | Joseph P. Wood

Etruscan Press Is Proud of Support Received From

Wilkes University

Youngstown State University

The Raymond John Wean Foundation

The Ohio Arts Council

The Stephen & Jeryl Oristaglio Foundation

The Nathalie & James Andrews Foundation

The National Endowment for the Arts

The Ruth H. Beecher Foundation

The Bates-Manzano Fund

The New Mexico Community Foundation

Founded in 2001 with a generous grant from the Oristaglio Foundation, Etruscan Press is a nonprofit cooperative of poets and writers working to produce and promote books that nurture the dialogue among genres, achieve a distinctive voice, and reshape the literary and cultural histories of which we are a part.

etruscan press

www.etruscanpress.org

Etruscan Press books may be ordered from

Consortium Book Sales and Distribution

800.283.3572

www.cbsd.com

Etruscan Press is a 501(c)(3) nonprofit organization.
Contributions to Etruscan Press are tax deductible
as allowed under applicable law.
For more information, a prospectus,
or to order one of our titles,
contact us at books@etruscanpress.org.